RIEKA HUNT

Of Lies and Shadows

Copyright © 2022 by Rieka Hunt

All rights reserved. No part of this publication may be reproduced, stored or transmitted in any form or by any means, electronic, mechanical, photocopying, recording, scanning, or otherwise without written permission from the publisher. It is illegal to copy this book, post it to a website, or distribute it by any other means without permission.

This novel is entirely a work of fiction. The names, characters and incidents portrayed in it are the work of the author's imagination. Any resemblance to actual persons, living or dead, events or localities is entirely coincidental.

First edition

Cover art by Paul Dovo

This book was professionally typeset on Reedsy. Find out more at reedsy.com

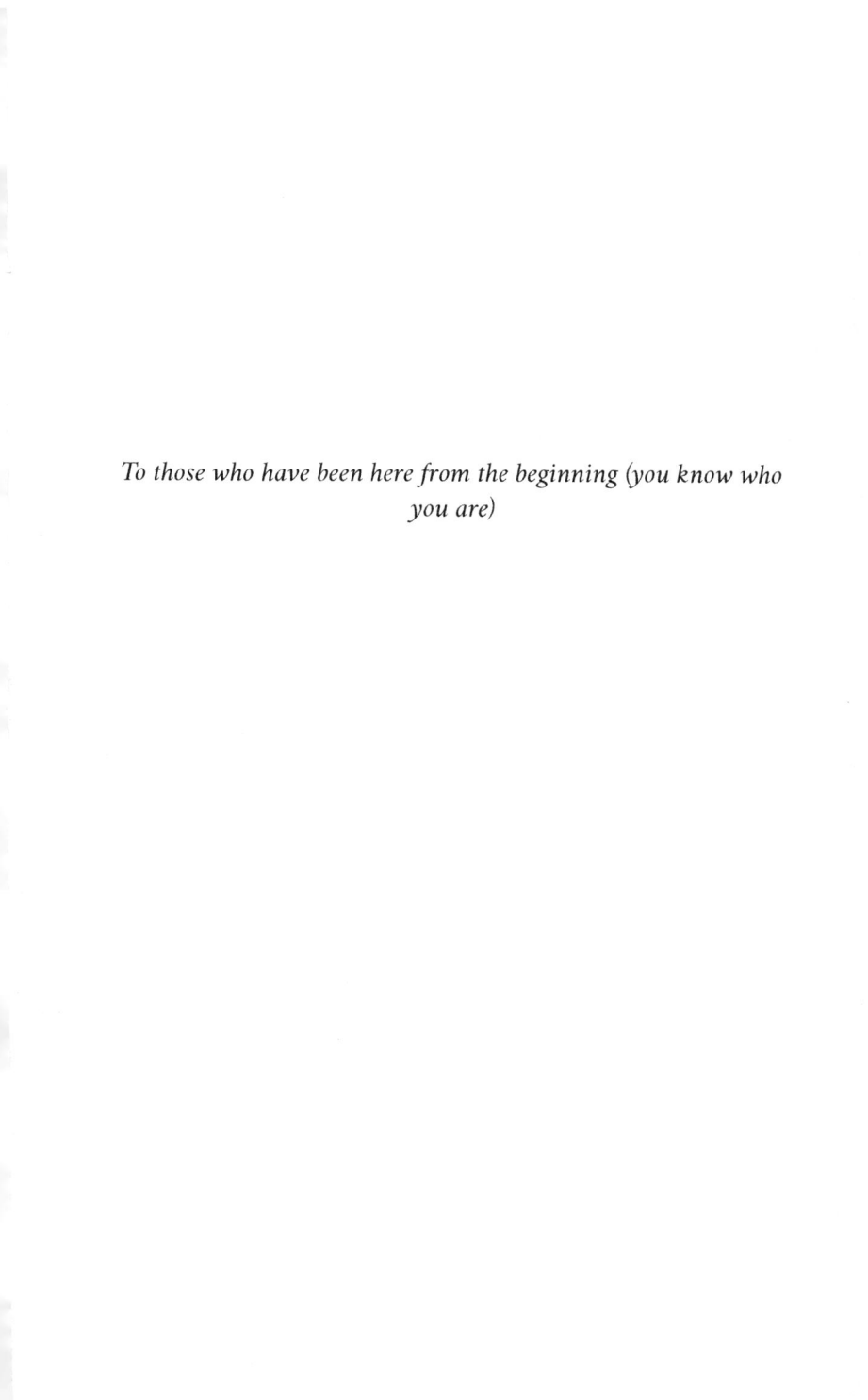

To those who have been here from the beginning (you know who you are)

Contents

Prologue	1
1.	3
2.	12
3.	19
4.	27
5.	35
6.	43
7.	49
8.	56
9.	64
10.	69
11.	77
12.	84
13.	91
14.	100
15.	108
16.	117
17.	124
18.	131
19.	139
20.	145
21.	152
22.	159
23.	165

24.	172
25.	179
26.	185
27.	192
28.	199
29.	205
Acknowledgments	209

Prologue

A cloaked figure stood at the edge of the woods watching guards from each Kingdom pick through the ruins of The Academy of Etrayus. They were looking through the rubble, searching for the remains of those who were crushed and killed when the buildings crumbled. Some students were able to escape on their own while others were able to thanks to teachers and staff. However, there were still plenty of people who weren't lucky enough to get out in time.

They focused mainly on the two dormitory buildings where the majority of the bodies would be. Their current orders were to locate any and all remains so they could begin identifying the victims. In the time this figure had stood here, they'd seen a few intact bodies pulled out. Other than that, though, they saw bits and pieces. An arm, a leg, or even just a finger were unearthed from the rubble.

The sun began to rise, casting a golden glow over the

wreckage. It doesn't always rain when tragedy strikes. The rays of the sun exposed the ominous clusters of dark energy drifting through the campus. They were a physical residue of magic that only appeared when immensely powerful spells or rituals were cast. Etryaus was home to magic users, most of whom were powerful in their own ways. Which, unfortunately, didn't narrow down the list of suspects.

The figure watched the guards for a little over an hour and decided they'd seen enough. With one last glance towards the wreck, then down to the body bags spread across the ground, they bowed their head reciting a silent prayer. The lone figure turned away from the scene and disappeared into a portal.

1.

"Feyre! If you don't get up right now, you'll be late for the meeting!"

Before I could respond, let alone react, my curtains were thrown open, flooding my room with sunlight. My blankets were soon ripped off me, too. I slowly opened my eyes already prepared to pick a fight.

"Oh." My eyes fell on the woman who had been my nanny for the last eighteen years. "Merindah."

She rolled her bright green eyes as she put her hands on her hips. "You need to get up and get dressed now. Your father made it *very* clear how upset he'd be if you were late."

That got me and my brain moving. Today was the public meeting about the academy attack. We'd spent weeks preparing for the best and worst-case scenarios, including a script for what each Council member would say in anticipation. After all of that work, I certainly wasn't going to risk missing this.

I jumped out of bed and made my way to my closet. "Do I need to dress formally?"

"Semi-formal, at least. I mean, the entire Council will be there," Merindah answered. A knock on my door stole her attention. "I'll get that, you get dressed."

I stepped into my closet and shut the door behind me. Alone,

I started going through my clothes. I skipped my pants entirely, thinking they would be too casual. I found myself skimming through my dresses instead. I needed to look like the Princess of Reidell, somehow, without wearing a full ballgown.

After spending a few minutes combing through my clothes, I landed on a midnight blue dress with a puffy princess skirt that stopped a few inches above my knees. It had thin straps made from sheer fabric that draped over my upper arms. It had a light blue belt with a lotus – my mother and I's favorite flower – embroidered on it. It was a dress my mother had made for me. It seemed only fitting that since she couldn't be at the meeting today, I should wear it.

I slipped on a pair of black stockings and stuffed my feet into heeled boots and walked out of my closet. Merindah pushed a muffin on a plate into my hands and began work on buttoning up the back of my dress. When she finished, she nudged me towards my vanity, leaving me to cram my muffin into my mouth.

"Are you going to walk, or would you like me to have your coach prepared?" Merindah asked.

"I'd rather walk," I answered, setting the now empty plate off to the side. "I'm sure the streets are going to be crowded with people, portals, and other coaches. It will be quicker and easier to walk."

I ran a quick brush through my ginger hair to get out all the knots. I swiped on a bit of mascara to make my blue eyes pop. I would've preferred to do a full face of makeup, but there simply wasn't enough time.

I jumped to my feet and Merindah pushed my cloak into my hands. It was a gift from Mother for my sixteenth birthday. It shifted from blue to black depending on the lighting, revealing

1.

that it was enchanted. The spell made it better suited for armor than a fashion statement. The clasp at the neck was a golden lotus.

She had it made when she and Father started letting me participate more in the everyday activities of a King and Queen. They both believed it was better to train me with a more hands-on approach but they were also concerned about danger. So, Mother had King Demir from the mountain Kingdom of Dradour make me this cloak.

"Do you really think I'll need it?" I asked, suddenly feeling nervous.

Merindah gave me a sad smile. "These are trying times."

I returned her sad smile and darted out of my room. I slipped out of the palace as quickly as I could and tried to not think too hard about what could happen today. However, I couldn't stop dwelling on Merindah's words. "These are trying times."

The Academy of Etrayus – where children from every city, town, and kingdom in this country went to learn about our history while training to control their magic – had been destroyed. We lost countless innocent lives that night. We had no idea who was behind the attack as no groups had come forward claiming responsibility and the evidence was leading us nowhere.

To make matters worse, we didn't really know what happened. Despite questioning countless witnesses and finding every minuscule piece of evidence we could, we were in the dark. Merindah truly hit the nail on the head.

These were trying times.

I reached the courthouse and felt my chest grow tight as I saw the crowd. There was a large line all the way down the sidewalk wrapping around the block. Coaches were still bringing more people to join and the familiar twinkles of portals opening could be heard all around. With so many people, a lot could go wrong before anyone could jump in and stop it.

I flicked the hood of my cloak up and kept my head down to hide my hair. Everyone told me I was a spitting image of my mother with my bright orange hair and blue eyes. I didn't need anyone mistaking me for her out here. Plus, the handful times I'd left the palace in the last few weeks, people had bombarded me demanding answers I didn't have. My guards had to arrest many of them.

Luckily, I was able to slip through the crowd and into the alleyway undetected. I made my way to the back entrance of the courthouse, where a guard was waiting.

"Princess Feyre," He smiled. "We weren't sure if you were still coming today since you didn't arrive with King Zander."

I returned his smile as I pulled my hood town. "I woke up a bit late."

He laughed softly as he opened the door. "Only you could sleep in on a day like this."

I grew serious, embarrassed – rightfully – by his assessment of me. "May the Gods and Goddesses watch over you all today."

He bowed. "Thank you, Princess."

I bee-lined for the conference room where the juries were typically put for deliberation. Father and the other Council members sat together idly chatting. With one quick look around the room, I noticed there were two very important people missing. Queen Morana, who ruled over Moroluma, the Kingdom of Darkness, and her heir, Drystan.

"Feyre, I was starting to think you wouldn't make it," Father said.

I curtsied to the other Council members. "I woke up late.

1.

Where are Queen Morana and Drystan?"

"We're unsure," Amara, Queen of Felluna, the Kingdom of life, answered.

Father sighed, "I hope she arrives soon. We can't start without her and I'm hesitant to start late…especially with that crowd out there."

"I told you we shouldn't depend on her," Demir stated. "Everyone who has ever ruled over Moroluma proves they can't be trusted for one reason or another."

"Every Kingdom gets a representative on Council; it's been that way since Etrayus was born," Father replied. Always diplomatic. Always following the rules.

Demir's mouth gaped open, ready to continue his protest, but a portal opened in the corner of the room interrupting him. Morana and Drystan stepped through, earning all of our attention – just as she liked.

"I apologize for our tardiness. We had a bit of a guard emergency this morning," Morana said. "Amara, you look beautiful."

She wasn't wrong. Amara's dark, tightly coiled hair was woven with flowers and pulled into a bun. The light, flowing green dress she wore matched her eyes and went perfectly with her dark skin. Everything about her contrasted with Morana. Morana's straight, dark hair was left down hanging limply around her pale face. Her brown eyes looked dull and her black dress was sleek and tight to her willowy body.

Amara grinned, "You do as well."

"If you were going to be late, you should have sent word," Demir said, annoyance evident in his voice.

"Now is not the time for this," Csilla, Queen of Artheas, our most ancient Kingdom, stated.

"Csilla's right. We need to be out there in a few minutes," Father said. "Now. Drystan, I secured a spot for you and a guard in the front row as Morana requested. Feyre, I sat you in the back. You're both close to exits so your guards can get you out if something goes wrong."

"Thank you, King Zander," Drystan said.

I gave Father a quick hug and made my way out into the packed courtroom. Drystan quickly found his seat while I was stuck elbowing my way through the crowd. I kept to the wall where the guards were standing. They helped me get to the back. I recognized a guard obnoxiously taking up two spots on the bench.

Alliard.

He was Father's personal guard but was assigned to me so frequently, I'm sure others thought he was mine. Today he was dressed in civillian clothes, which was strange for me to see. I don't think I'd ever seen him look so casual before. If it weren't for the standard guard haircut which kept his chocolate brown hair buzzed on the sides and longer on the top, he looked like any other citizen.

"Princess Feyre, nice to see you again," Alliard said quietly as I took my seat next to him.

"I should've known that Father would assign you to me today."

Alliard grinned, "He knows I'm your favorite guard."

"You're simply the least irritating," I teased.

He lightly bumped my elbow into my arm while I bit back a laugh. After a moment, I watched his face grow serious.

"What do you think about all this?" he asked.

"It was a deliberate attack. They knew exactly what they were doing."

1.

Our conversation was cut off by the Council, who began taking their seats. Within seconds, everyone in the courtroom stopped their conversation leaving it eerily silent.

"We're here today to discuss The Academy of Etrayus being attacked as well as our ongoing investigation. We will do our best to put your minds at ease today, but please remember that this is an ongoing investigation so we cannot disclose all the information and evidence we have," Father said.

Amara spoke next, "After we tell you everything, we will open the floor to anyone who has any questions or concerns they would like to voice."

"With that, let us begin our findings," Demir said. "We know the people behind this were a large, organized, and powerful group. They were able to shatter the wards surrounding the campus and take out the guards patrolling the perimeter. They were then able to disable the alarms, which, of course, left everyone unsure if it was a malfunction, test, or drill."

"We're working on trying to compare this attack and the evidence we found to any other crimes that have happened in recent years in hopes of being able to create a list of suspects. So far we don't have any, but we are only at the beginning of this process," Csilla said.

"We know everyone has been asking for a list of victims and survivors, but we don't have that yet. There are many students and faculty who are unaccounted for and bodies who haven't been identified yet. As for those we *have* identified, the families have asked us to not release their names so they can grieve in peace," Morana said.

The majority haven't been identified because all they could find was a limb or two. Some, however, we hadn't even found a single fingernail for. It was heartbreaking.

"We know this isn't a lot of information, but this is all we can give at this time. We hope you can understand," Father implored. "We will now open the floor to anyone who would like to speak."

No one moved or rose from their seats – all was quiet. Slowly, an older man at the front of the crowd got to his feet and strode toward the podium.

"We have been waiting for three weeks for you to say something! Three weeks! And this is all you have for us? This is all you have to say?" he shouted. "Children are dead! *Our* children are dead! And whoever did this is out there in Etrayus walking free!"

This received a lot of cheers and support. Others shouted over one another, expressing their shared outrage. I gripped the hem of my dress as fear and anger bubbled up in my chest. They were losing the crowd which could be dangerous.

I could see Csilla and Father trying to speak, likely in an attempt to calm the crowd, but they were quickly drowned out. Now everyone was standing, screaming, and demanding more answers. Guards quickly jumped into action, trying to quiet the crowd or get them back in their seats. No one listened. The crowd pushed toward Council.

Without warning, Alliard pulled me to my feet and started dragging me towards the exit. I fought against him, staring horrified over my shoulder. I tried to get a glimpse of Father. Alliard was a lot stronger than I was. He managed to drag me out of there with minimal effort.

"All guards into the courthouse! They've lost control of the crowd!" Alliard shouted to the guards still posted outside.

They were quick to action and hurriedly disappeared inside to assist with the chaos. Realizing resistance was pointless,

1.

I obediently followed Alliard as he walked us to a coach. He helped me inside and ordered the driver to take us to the palace. Within seconds, we were speeding through the empty streets toward home.

2.

We arrived at the palace, and Alliard was still tense. He gathered some guards as he led me to my room. From there, Alliard and I would be locked in until he got word things were safe. I couldn't help but roll my eyes.

"This all seems a bit...extreme," I said.

"I've seen people go to extremes in order to get what they want. As you're the only heir to Reidell, we aren't going to take any risks with you," Alliard replied.

I got myself comfortable on my bed knowing I was going to be here for a while. I'd known Alliard for two years and knew better than to argue with him or try to sweet-talk him into doing what I wanted.

About half an hour of painstaking silence ticked by before a knock came at my door. I practically leaped off my bed, but one firm look from Alliard was enough to stop me in my tracks. With one hand on his sword, he cautiously opened the door. Looking over his shoulder, a wave of relief washed over me as I saw Merindah standing there. Without hesitation, she pushed past Alliard into the room, then pulled me into a tight hug.

"Zander wishes to see you and Alliard in the War Room," she said as she released me, wasting no time getting down to business.

2.

"He wants me there?" Alliard asked, confused.

Merindah nodded. "You are still in charge of watching our precious Feyre, after all."

"Thank you, Merindah," I said, giving her another quick hug.

I grabbed Alliard by the wrist and led him down to the basement where the War Room was hidden. We weaved through storage boxes and unused decorations until we reached the back corner.

"This isn't as glamorous as I was expecting," Alliard admitted.

I laughed. "The outside isn't supposed to be glamorous. It's supposed to be well hidden. It also acts as a safe room."

"How do you open the door? I can't even see the seam for it."

"Blood."

As an aether user, I was able to use raw magic energy in my body and the air around me to craft essentially whatever I wanted. Weapons and creatures were my main specialty. With the correct training, which I had thanks to Amara, I was also able to cauterize wounds and cleanse some poisons and infections from the body. It was a rare magic to have as it was a divine ability like angelic light.

I formed an aether dagger in my hand, then dug the tip into one of my fingers. When blood began to pool, I let the dagger vanish as I smeared my blood into the center of the spelled area. The illusion dropped, revealing a metal door with a dorioya tree, the symbol of Etrayus, carved into the center.

I looked over my shoulder at Alliard and he looked nervous, if not a little nauseated.

"Don't look so freaked out," I said. "You're one of the King's personal guards, you were bound to see this room sooner or later."

Not giving him a chance to respond, I pushed open the heavy

door revealing the War Room. Maps of Etrayus and each Kingdom covered one wall and large bookcases took over the other. The most interesting feature was the wooden round table where the Council sat. It had a detailed map of Etrayus burned into the wood. It marked every minor feature, like the mountain ranges where Dradour sat or The Infected Lands of Moroluma. My favorite, though, had to be all the towns tucked away in forests. Most didn't know they existed unless they lived there.

Father got to his feet and pulled me into a tight hug, pressing my face into his chest. His beard tickled my skin as he pressed a kiss to my forehead. When he released me, he turned his attention to Alliard. "You did well today, Alliard."

"I was only doing my job, King Zander," Alliard said, bowing slightly.

With a grateful smile, Father motioned to the table, "Please, join us."

"What happened?" I asked as I took my seat.

"Nothing too bad. The guards were able to get us out of there and gain control over the crowd. We did hear that a few citizens were injured in the chaos and had to be taken to the hospital, but none were life-threatening," Amara answered.

"The more important question is what the hell are we supposed to do now," Morana said. "They aren't going to let up until someone's at least arrested."

Father let out a sigh, running his hand through his hair. The dark strands that were once perfectly slicked back fell out of place.

"I'm considering requesting the Elder join our investigation."

"You can't be serious!" Morana exclaimed.

"In what world would they help us?" Demir asked, his shock

2.

blending with Morana's.

"We've been trying to piece together the evidence we do have and have tried searching the campus for additional evidence for weeks now. We have no answers, and our tests have led us nowhere. At least the Elders have a chance at deciphering magic energies and they could assist in identifying disembodied limbs," Father explained.

"I might have to agree with Demir and Morana on this," Amara said. "There's no way they would help us."

"They aren't as heartless as you all might think," Csilla stated, hiding behind her white-blond hair, as if embarrassed.

The Elders were essentially Gods and Goddesses to us. They were the ones that created Etrayus thousands of years ago and were part of the reason we were all alive today. However, they locked themselves away in the Artheas Temple for us to worship them, but never to be interacted with. When something happened, they didn't step in to assist and were notorious for refusing to give us a drop of their wisdom. Over thousands of years, only about three instances have been documented of them assisting with investigations.

"They'll help us because children were slaughtered," I stated.

Father smiled, beaming proudly at my words. "Feyre's right. They'll care because of the children, which could affect the one thing they care about: Etrayus' future."

"Let Csilla ask them to help. She can butter them up," Morana suggested.

"As much as I'd love to do that, they only take formal requests for things like this," Csilla replied.

"So we'll spend all that time filling out packets of paper for them to say no," Morana said.

"If they say no-"

"They will," Demir muttered.

"If they say no," Father started again. "We'll continue doing what we can on our own. It wouldn't be ideal, but we'll figure it out like we always do."

Father paused to see if anyone had any further complaints or protests. No one did.

"Alright. Now Alliard, I am assigning you to be Feyre's personal guard until further notice. I expect you to by her side at all hours of the day."

Alliard nodded. "Yes, sir."

"You don't trust me to be alone?" I asked innocently.

It was Demir who broke out into a laugh first, his round belly shaking. My Father followed suit.

"Feyre, we all love you, but we also know all the trouble you've gotten yourself into in only eighteen years of life," Amara said, grinning.

"You're worse than your mother ever was," Father said once he was able to stop laughing.

That got another round of chuckles, but this time everyone joined in. It felt nice to have a small moment of joy to ease the ache of the chaos and fear that had taken over Etrayus.

"Feyre, Alliard, and Drystan are dismissed. Everyone else, we should discuss how we're going to convince the Elders to assist us," Father said.

I said my goodbyes to everyone before walking out with Alliard following close behind. We were silent as we made our way back up to my bedroom, both lost in our own thoughts.

I was relieved to see that everyone who has previously been in my room was now gone. Alliard and I would be able to talk privately.

"Tell me about what's going on in that head of yours," I said as soon as the door was closed.

Alliard sighed, shaking his head. "I just- I'm not quite sure what I just heard. I'm not used to being part of meetings, and I don't entirely know the inner workings of Etrayus." He stopped talking abruptly, taking a moment to collect himself before continuing, "I just don't understand why we'd have to jump through all these hoops to get the Elders to help. Why do we need to submit a formal request when they could offer help themselves?"

"The Elders are the equivalent of grandparents. They've done their duty of building and growing Etrayus and they don't want to have to do it again. They'll offer support and words of wisdom, but from a distance and when it suits them. To them, we should be able to maintain this country without them," I said. "Because of that, they're extremely picky. They don't want us running to them for assistance every time we can't figure it out ourselves."

"But they care about the future of Etrayus," Alliard spoke slowly.

"They worked hard to build Etrayus from the ground up. They don't want it ruined or destroyed, especially not because of some psychotic group who enjoys murdering children."

"Why didn't the Council try to bring them in from the beginning, then?" Alliard asked.

"Honestly? I don't know." I shook my head. "Part of me thinks that something new has come to light or something has changed. Something important enough for Father to be worried about us not being able to do it without them. That's just my assumption, though, I don't really know if anything has happened. I haven't seen all the evidence they've found."

At the end of the day, all that matters is that we get justice for those who lost their lives. It didn't matter if the Council did it themselves or if it was thanks to the Elders' assistance. Justice was all that mattered. Now, if word got out that Father was even considering asking the Elders for help, all hell would break loose.

People were already upset that we didn't have suspects or answers yet. Through their frustration, they were still hopeful and believed this would all be resolved soon. If word got out that Council decided to bring in the Elders, it would terrify them even more. There would be more panic and fear through Etrayus if that happened…things were surely only going to get worse.

3.

The last few days have been filled with nothing but tension and stress. Protesters were outside the palace non-stop now. They could be heard screaming and demanding answers keeping some of us awake at night. Every few hours, guards would break up the crowds that had formed. The first day, day-and-a-half, no one argued or tried to pick fights. Last night, however, a group of people tried to rush the guards to get onto the palace grounds.

This morning, we posted guards at the gates to ward off any returning protesters. Because of this, those that did try to return caused a lot of chaos as well as started a lot of fights. This led to them being arrested. It was bound to continue to happen throughout the day. This would leave me locked up for the night with no chance of sneaking out. Another night of doing nothing for me was going to drive me insane.

What made it all worse was that Father had confined himself away into his office. He's been in there since the Council had finished discussing bringing the Elders in for help a few days ago. According to Merindah and other staff members, he went from the War Room straight into his office. He'd been eating and sleeping in there as he worked tirelessly on the formal request to send to the Elders. He only emerged to use the bathroom.

It was infuriating, to say the least. The guards were working overtime in an attempt to keep the peace in Reidell and Merindah was doing everything in her power to help keep the palace running while Father ignored it all. I wanted nothing more than to barge in there and order him out like Mother would, but I knew better than to try that when he got like this. It would only end in an argument and me leaving, feeling defeated.

All of this led to me sitting in one of the upstairs parlors listening to Merindah drone on about etiquette at royal events. It felt like the last thing I needed or wanted to be concerned about because I didn't know the next time I'd need this information, but I understood why Merindah was doing it. She was trying to keep some sense of normalcy around here which was something we all needed.

I tried to give her my attention, but it was hard to stay focused. Even Alliard, who was standing off to the side of the room, was struggling to stay awake.

"Queen Calla!" Merindah exclaimed excitedly, jarring me back to reality. "We weren't expecting you to be back until next week."

Mother had been away in Felluna, her home Kingdom, for the last couple of weeks. She'd been assisting Amara's research teams on a project breeding exotic plants from The Enchanted Forest. A lot of the plants in the forest are used to create powerful medicinal potions. Because of that, they've been trying to figure out a way to get them to grow outside of The Enchanted Forest. The magic that flows through Etrayus is powerful. It's what allows us all to use our magic without any limitations. However, it's more concentrated in the forest due to rituals and a lot of tender care making it better suited for growing these exotic plants without any issues.

They wanted to use life magic and rituals throughout Etrayus to make patches of concentrated magic on the same level as The Enchanted Forest. It sounded simple enough, but Mother said it was a long, complex process. Even with the most powerful biomancers – who could create life from nothing – working on it they were having trouble figuring it out.

"Amara filled me in on what was happening, so I knew I had to rush back to make sure Zander hadn't fallen into one of his pits," Mother responded.

"He's been locked away in the office for days now. He's left the guards to figure out how to deal with all the protesters without any assistance," I grumbled.

Mother let out an exasperated sigh. "Merindah, would you mind having someone bring us some tea? It seems Feyre has a few things of her own to tell me."

"Of course!" Merindah smiled. She gave Mother another quick hug and said, "It's wonderful to have you home." Before rushing off.

"Alliard, dear, you don't have to hide away in the corner. Come sit with us; it looks like you could use the rest."

Alliard looked conflicted for a moment but quickly sat on the couch across from ours. However, he didn't let himself sink in and get comfortable. He sat on the edge, visibly ready to jump up if anything happened.

"Is what Amara said true? Is your father writing up a request for the Elders to join the investigation?" Mother asked.

"He seems desperate. He convinced everyone on Council to at least keep their negativity about it to themselves."

Mother shook her head. "I can't believe I had to hear about

all of this from Amara. Even what happened at the courthouse I heard from her! Can you believe that!"

"I assumed he'd sent you a letter or something, considering how long he's been in the office."

Merindah stepped back into the room holding a tray with a teapot, cups, and all the fixings. She set it on the table and took a seat next to Alliard. We paused, tending to our drinks before returning to the topic at hand.

"He hasn't let the maids in there, so who knows what it looks like," Merindah commented.

"Has he even been out to bathe?" Mother asked.

Merindah laughed. "That man has barely come out to use the bathroom."

That seemed to set Mother over the edge. Scowling, she got to her feet with her teacup in hand.

"If you will excuse me, it seems I have a husband to deal with."

I bit back a laugh, watching Mother leave the parlor. Merindah stayed for a few minutes to finish her tea before excusing herself, leaving Alliard and me alone. We sat silently, both enjoying our tea, unsure of what to do. I was supposed to be in this lesson until lunch.

"I always forget that you and Queen Calla look identical," Alliard said, breaking the silence.

"Yeah, I'm definitely my mother's child," I agreed, smiling.

"Your hair is even the same shade of orange. It's a bit eerie, honestly."

"That's something she likes to brag about a lot. She and Father sometimes have mock arguments about it."

I went quiet for a moment, then asked, "Can I ask you something?"

He laughed. "Technically you just did, but sure."

"So I've been stuck in the palace for a few days, as you know. Well, as I've been walking around, I've been hearing some of the guards gossiping about you. They all seem to be jealous or judgmental," I said. "I guess what I want to know is, is this normal? Is it normal for guards to be as catty as girls can be when someone gets a sought-after position or job?"

Alliard nodded. "It's a pretty normal thing, unfortunately. I saw it a lot even when I was just a guard in a small town, but ever since becoming one of King Zander's guards, it's gotten worse. Some try to act like we're best friends and then will ask me to pass on recommendations. Others are just passive-aggressive and moody."

"A lot were talking about you being assigned as my guard though. I thought no one wanted to be a Prince or Princesses guard."

"Typically it's one of the worst jobs. It's a lot of lessons, shopping, and listening to drama. You, however, are a special case. You're an only child. That means you're guaranteed a spot on a throne, which means whoever is assigned to you now has a pretty damn good chance at being your guard when you're crowned Queen."

"I never really thought about it like that," I admitted.

"There's also the fact that I was fortunate enough to become one of the youngest guards to ever be assigned to a King. A lot of guards would kill to be in my position at age forty or fifty and here I am freshly twenty-one and I'm at the top of my career."

"You're certainly not an average guard, that's for sure."

"Now, if you don't mind, I have a question. But this one might be a bit too personal or out of line," Alliard said.

I shrugged. "Ask away."

"Does King Zander often lock himself away for days on end?"

"I don't know if I'd say that he does it often, but he's done it enough that everyone knows how to handle it when it does happen. Mother says it's because he has a one-track mind when things go wrong. With how stubborn he can be...well, it creates this," I answered. "Mother is always around, though, to pick up the slack and to pull him back to reality when he's been checked out for too long."

"Sounds like a certain someone I know," Alliard teased.

"Who?" I asked, playing dumb.

"Just some girl I know," he said, leaning back into the couch. "I don't think you'd know her. She's way cooler than you."

I scoffed, "No one's cooler than me."

He shrugged, taking a sip of his tea. That pushed us over the edge into a fit of laughter.

~~~~~~~~~~~~~~~

It wasn't until I walked into the dining room for dinner that I saw Mother again. Father was in his chair at the head of the table. His hair still looked a bit damp, telling me Mother had helped him finish his task and ushered him to clean himself up.

"Where's Alliard?" Mother asked as I took my seat across from her.

"In the barracks. He wanted to get a few hours of sleep before tonight," I replied.

"He should join us for dinner one of these days. Goddess knows he's earned it," Mother sighed.

"I'll pass on the invitation."

Servers brought dinner out to us, and Father all but began inhaling it. It didn't even seem like he was chewing.

3.

"So, what's the update?" I asked.

"We've written up a proper request to send to the Elders. We've condensed all the evidence we have as well as witness testimonies hoping it will demonstrate to them how serious this is and how desperate we are for their help," Mother answered.

"Do we really need their help that badly?" I asked.

"There are things we haven't told you, Feyre, that made this whole thing...odd, to say the least," Father explained.

"But you've always told me everything," I said, feeling betrayed.

Even before I started being allowed to be involved in Council meetings and such, they'd openly talk about what was happening with me at dinner or breakfast. Sometimes they'd specifically call me into the office to talk to me about what was going on. They used each instance as a way to teach me about paperwork, how to talk to people, how to phrase questions, and so on. To hear that they were intentionally keeping something from me, it hurt.

"It isn't because we don't trust you," Mother quickly explained. "It's because we can't risk some of this information getting out."

"You've never worried about that before," I argued.

All the staff in the palace have been around since my parents got married and began ruling Reidell together. They handpicked everyone who worked here and ran extensive background checks on everyone to ensure they could be trusted. Through the years, we've all become a tight-knit family. My parents never worried about anyone overhearing things because they never worried about them leaking information.

"We have no idea what we've found or what's going on.

Whatever it is, it isn't good. We aren't taking any risks on this getting out and don't want to discuss it outside of a secure room," Mother said.

If they were truly worried about it getting out to the point where they weren't willing to discuss it with me, it explained why they wanted the Elders in on this. It had to be something significant.

It was clear they didn't have any intentions of telling me about what it was anytime soon. I'd need to figure it out on my own. The only way to do that would be to do my own investigation and walkthrough of the academy campus.

It seemed I had to find a way to sneak out tonight, after all.

4.

Night quickly fell over Etrayus. The palace was mostly quiet aside from the occasional footsteps of guards or night staff making their rounds. It was the perfect time to sneak out.

I slipped into my closet, exchanging my dress and heels for pants, a tunic, and boots. It was more suitable attire for exploring the academy grounds and the woods that surrounded it. I gathered my hair into a ponytail as Alliard walked into my room ready for his night shift of guarding me.

"Why are you getting all dressed up?" Alliard asked.

"We're going on an adventure," I said, smiling.

"King Zander and Queen Calla don't want you leaving the palace."

"And if I do need to leave the palace I'm supposed to take you with me. Which I am."

The internal argument he was having with himself was written all over his face. After a minute, he seemed to give in.

"Fine. But we need to be back well before sunrise," Alliard relented.

"All I need is an hour or two," I replied, beaming.

"Something tells me I'm going to regret this," he muttered.

Ignoring him, I formed a ball of aether and pressed it into the wall opening a portal. The familiar twinkle of a successful portal floated through my ears.

Portal magic was one of the most important but basic magics out there. As long as you had your magic, a wall or door, and a location in mind you'd be able to form a portal. The hardest part was keeping your location clear in your mind while you did it, otherwise your portal could fizzle out or you'd end up far away from your intended destination.

I turned around, wrapped my hand around Alliard's wrist, and pulled him through the swirling, glittery doorway. We stepped out finding ourselves at the entrance of the academy. The full moon hung overhead providing adequate lighting so we could see everything around us. The administrative building was still standing and appeared to be entirely untouched. However, energy masses could be seen drifting through the air sending a chill down my spine.

"Feyre. Why are we here?" Alliard asked slowly.

"Tonight at dinner my parents told me there are things they haven't told me. I need answers and this campus is where I'm going to find them."

My mind took me back to the early hours after the attack. Guards picked through the rubble, looking for bodies only to pull out a disembodied arm or leg. Energy masses floating through the campus, weaving through demolished buildings.

I had been desperate to get a closer look and maybe help search for evidence. I couldn't help then, but I could now."

"We shouldn't be here. We could taint evidence or disturb something important," Alliard hissed.

I shook my head. "They got everything they could out of this place. Even if they didn't, it's not like I'm going to go around touching everything. I just want to walk around and take a look at things for myself."

"Feyre really-"

My eyes snapped to his. "You're more than welcome to go back to the palace and hang out in my room until I get back, but I'm not leaving here until I have answers."

Without waiting for a response, I started walking down the sidewalk along the side of the administrative building leading to the rest of the campus. I didn't get very far before something grabbed my attention. On the brick wall, there were four deep slashes. They looked like claw marks.

I heard Alliard approach, but I couldn't tear my eyes away from the gouges. Etrayus didn't have many large creatures and there certainly weren't any that would be capable of doing something like this.

"Wha...what could have made those?" Alliard asked in a hushed voice.

"I have no idea."

Creating a small orb of aether, I let it drift closer to the wall so the glow could allow me to get a better look. There appeared to be some sort of sheer, black goo within the gouges.

"My parents never mentioned this," I said.

"How could they?" Alliard responded. "There's no explanation for that. Nothing in Etrayus should be able to do this."

"I think I'm already starting to understand why Father wants to bring the Elders in."

Slowly, I pulled myself away from the wall. I wanted to search the campus and see if there were more secrets to be unearthed. Alliard stayed in step with me, making sure to be at my side as I continued my exploration.

I knew the two dormitory buildings were destroyed. Seeing

the buildings that once held classrooms half demolished and crumbling made my chest tight. Those were halls I had once walked and classrooms that I had sat in. Now there was nothing.

I'd heard the agriculture building at the very back of the campus had been leveled and the garden built there had been trampled. Staff buildings had gotten the same treatment. Whoever did this seemed to want everything gone.

It wasn't until we reached the center of campus when I began seeing the bulk of the energy masses. The power radiating off of them was overwhelming. My head throbbed and my stomach turned when I wandered too close to them.

"Are they all dark energy?" Alliard asked as one drifted by him.

"I'm not sure," I frowned. "Reading energies was something I elected to not learn since it's a dying skill."

"So we can't say for sure that Moroluma was behind this."

I looked at him, knitting my eyebrows together, "Where did that come from?"

"We all know that people from Moroluma are nothing but troublemakers. It's not much of a leap to think that they could be behind this."

He had a point. Moroluma was seen as the rotten egg of the Kingdoms. They were the stain on our history. If you were a resident of Moroluma, you were seen as evil as the man who created the land it sat on. A man named Delroy – one of the founders of Etrayus.

The story goes that he experimented with dark magic as well as human and animal sacrifices. As a result of that experimentation, he managed to infect the land itself. It killed every living thing in that area, but it amplified his powers

4.

when he was on the land, so he deemed it a success. However, it began spreading to the point where it could have put Felluna at risk. So, the other Elders banded together and created the most powerful wards anyone had ever seen. It was enough to block the dark magic from spreading.

After Delroy's execution, the Elders wanted to do something with the land. So, they chose to create Moroluma in an attempt to turn something negative into a positive. Because of this, Moroluma didn't exactly have a set purpose like the other Kingdoms.

Felluna specialized in earth and life. They grew our plants and crops, created potions and medicines, and overall did their best to make life in Etrayus beautiful and worthwhile. Artheas, our most ancient Kingdom, invented enchantments and technology while keeping our older ways of life alive. Dradour held out architects and blacksmiths. They helped build and maintain every town and Kingdom in Etrayus. They also took the enchantments created by Artheas to make our weapons and armor more powerful. And Reidell was our capital. It gave us common ground and represented everyone coming together as one powerful country.

"No one in Etrayus can be ruled out or targeted," I stated.

We arrived at the courtyard, which appeared to be mostly untouched. All the benches and tables were intact. The trees around the perimeter to give the area shade were all still standing. Then my eyes landed on the courtyard's main feature, the dorioya tree. It towered over everything, including the buildings.

Dorioya trees were the symbol of Etrayus' power. They fed off the pure, raw magic energy that flowed through the land, which allowed them to grow as large as they did. The trunk was thick and twisted as if two or three trees had fused together. The branches were large and covered in beautiful silver leaves that glowed even during the day. It grew fruits called dorioya berries that were about the size of apples. They were sweet but tart and when eaten, they amplified your powers for a short period of time.

This one, however, looked wrong. That beautiful glow was barely there and it's typically strong magical energy felt weak.

"Look," Alliard said, pointing up at the branches. "It's fighting off the energy masses."

I narrowed my eyes and started up at the branches. It wasn't long before I could see what he was talking about. When one of the energy masses got too close, it would expel a bright burst of energy. The energy mass would either explode into a light fog before disappearing, killing it or it would send the mass soaring across the courtyard. The tree was defending itself.

"I didn't know they could do that," I said, awed.

"Me either," Alliard gasped.

I cautiously made my way toward the tree, wanting to get a closer look. Creating a few aether orbs, I flung them upwards so they could illuminate the tree. I gasped when the lights cast shadows over the deep cuts on the trunk. They were about as big as the claw marks on the wall. Whatever did that had attacked the tree.

I let my fingers graze one of the cuts, causing the dorioya tree to release a large burst of energy directed at me. It sent me flying across the courtyard. I hit the ground hard. The landing knocked all the air out of my lungs, leaving me lying on the ground, struggling to figure out how to breathe again. Alliard appeared at my side and he helped me into a sitting position, forcing me to put my head between my knees.

4.

"Deep breaths," he said calmly. "Slow, deep breaths."

I did as he said, and after a few agonizing moments, I was able to re-inflate my lungs.

"Thank you," I whispered.

We stayed that way until I could begin breathing normally again. Once Alliard was sure I was alright, he slowly helped me to my feet.

"Are you alright to keep going or do we need to head back?" he asked.

"I thought you wanted to go back, anyway," I smirked.

He smiled slightly in return, "I'll admit, all of this has caught my attention."

"I want to look at the dorioya tree again."

His smile dropped. "That thing just threw you like you were a rag doll and you want to get close to it again?"

"I need to try something."

"You need to—hey!"

Before he could finish speaking, I was already walking towards the tree again. This time I climbed up onto the planter so I was more level with its injuries. Gently resting my hand over the wounds, I let aether flow out of my hands into the tree. It resisted my magic at first, but once it realized what I was doing, it accepted my offering. I wanted to heal the tree completely but I didn't think I'd be able to physically handle that. Still, I was going to try.

My magic spilled freely until I grew lightheaded and dizzy. The tree had started glowing again. I slowly stemmed the flow of aether until it stopped entirely.

I turned around and went to hop off the planter feeling proud of myself. The world around me started spinning causing me to lose my balance and fall forward. I braced myself to hit the ground, but Alliard was there to catch me.

"I think that's enough for tonight," he said.

I nodded, exhausted, "Thank you…again."

He gently set me on my feet, making sure I wouldn't topple over again. He opened a portal, then wrapped an arm around my waist, helping me walk through into the safety of my bedroom.

No one was standing in my room waiting for us. There were no signs that anyone had been in here looking for us. I breathed a sigh of relief as the nervousness of getting caught evaporated.

"Did you get the answers you were looking for?" Alliard asked.

"Not at all," I replied, as I sat on my bed. "If anything, I'm more confused than I was before, and I can't even ask my parents about any of it."

"I'm sure they're just as confused as we are." he comforted.

Letting out a small sigh, I replied, "That's what I'm worried about."

5.

I awoke early the next morning. My mind was still reeling from what happened last night. Needing more time to process and not feeling ready to face my parents, I decided to lock myself in my room today. I needed to be alone.

I dragged myself out of bed and peaked my head out of my bedroom door. Alliard was leaning against the wall, barely managing to keep his head up.

"Head back to the barracks and get some rest. I'll be in my room today, so there's no real reason for you to be here," I said.

Alliard yawned. "Are you actually going to stay in your room or are you going to sneak off somewhere the second I leave?"

"I need time to wrap my head around what we saw last night, so trust me, I'll be glued to my room," I said. He looked hesitant, earning my sigh. "You need the day off to rest. Anyone with eyes can see that. I promise you won't get in any trouble, especially since I'm the one making the order."

"If you need anything or you have the urge to leave, have someone come wake me."

I rolled my eyes. "You're off duty for the day, accept it and go crawl into bed."

He stared at me undoubtedly preparing some sort of argument. But instead, he dropped his head in defeat and shuffled down the hallway. I watched him until he disappeared around the corner and down the stairs. I then slipped back into my room and drew myself a hot bath.

By the time I grabbed a fresh set of clothes from my closet, the tub was full. I stripped down, then let my body sink into the scalding water. Almost instantaneously, my body relaxed and I could think a bit more clearly. The things we saw last night were odd, but the dorioya tree was what stuck out the most.

Dorioya trees were protected by our laws. Everyone learned their history during their time in the academy, ensuring everyone knew what they represented. Whoever was behind this was trying to send some sort of message.

All of it only made me that much more curious about who was behind this. Slaughtering children was heinous enough, but they didn't stop there. They attempted to injure or kill a symbol of our country. What message were they trying to send? What was their end goal?

A loud knock on my bedroom door pulled me out of my thoughts. I tried to ignore it, hoping my silence would send my visitor away. But the knocking continued, cutting my bath — and my dwelling — short. I hastily got out of the tub and wrapped my robe around my body. A quiet string of curses and threats left my mouth as I stomped over to my door.

I swung it open fully prepared to rip into my untimely visitor when I saw my father standing there.

"I ran into Alliard while he was heading back to the barracks," he said. "I know you wouldn't willingly choose to stay inside the palace until something was going on."

"Protesters are still a problem, meaning there's nowhere I can really go, anyway," I replied.

5.

"When has something like that ever stopped you?"

I shrugged. "After our conversation last night, I figured I'd spare you and Mother the worry of me running around and possibly getting myself into trouble."

"Can I come in?" he asked.

I stepped to the side, motioning him through the doorway. He walked through and pulled my vanity bench with a scrape toward the center of the room. I perched myself on the edge of my bed, doing my best to appear cool, calm, and collected. Inside, I was panicking.

"You've been to the academy, haven't you?"

I tried to school my expression, suppressing the shockwave that thrummed through my body. My mind raced, as I thought of the best way to approach this. I could deny it. Insist that I didn't know what he was talking about. I could ask where he got such an idea from. I already knew the response—it was a well-loved adage of his. "I don't ask questions I don't already know the answer to."

I relented, "I have."

"When?"

"Last night, after everyone went to bed. I took Alliard with me."

"What did you see?"

"The claw marks on buildings. The weird goo in the scratches. All the energy masses. The dorioya tree."

Father nodded, then spoke only a hair above a whisper, "The claw marks are what we've been keeping from everyone. No one knows what could have done it."

"Not even Amara knows?"

"She's been searching any and every book on creatures in Etrayus as well as those that can be summoned. So far she's come up empty-handed. She's still searching, but it isn't looking like we'll be getting answers anytime soon."

"That's why you want to bring the Elders in," I said.

"It is. I'm hoping that they'll either know what did it or they'll be able to help us figure it out," he replied. "Did you touch or disrupt anything?"

"Not that I know of," I said slowly.

"What did you do?" he asked.

I bit the inside of my cheek. I wasn't thinking when I healed the dorioya tree, but by healing it, I might have destroyed evidence. At the very least, I tampered with it. Either way, it definitely wasn't a good thing, even if I did have good intentions.

"What. Did. You. Do?" Father repeated, his anger bleeding into every syllable.

"I-I healed the dorioya tree," I said. "Or – at least I tried to. I'm not sure how successful I was."

"You did what?" he snapped.

"It-it was suffering! Most likely dying! I couldn't just leave it there knowing it was dying! I had to do something!"

"Do you have any idea what you've done?" he asked, raising his voice. "Do you?"

"I-"

"You tampered with evidence! Evidence that we needed the Elders to look at and see for themselves!"

"But I just—"

"I don't want to hear whatever excuses you're trying to come up with, Feyre!" he ground out through gritted teeth.

I didn't try to argue. I knew what I did wasn't right. I understood wholly why he was upset.

"If you'll excuse me, I need to go see what damage you've

caused."

Father stood abruptly and was out my door before I could reply. I could feel the tears building as my cheeks grew warm with embarrassment. His anger was enough to make me second guess my decision. I knew I had good intentions, and I knew that losing the tree would make people even more heartbroken. It was stupid. Had I taken even a single second to think about what I was doing, I could have avoided all of this.

Gripping the edge of my robe tightly, I took a few deep breaths to collect myself. No tears fell and the feeling of embarrassment faded. There was no point in letting Father or his anger get to me. What's done is done. I couldn't change it now. The only thing I could hope for was that I hadn't messed things up too badly.

With one more deep breath, I got my feet. Glancing at my clock, I saw that breakfast should be done soon. I stepped into my closet and dressed for the day. After that, I spent a bit of time at my vanity then headed down to the dining room.

I wholeheartedly expected to be dining alone this morning. Instead, I was met with Mother sitting in her usual spot across from mine. My stomach dropped to my feet and my palms grew sweaty.

Under normal circumstances, I'd be overjoyed to see her. No, though, all I could think about was how Father had likely already told her what had happened. It had only been twenty minutes or so since our conversation, but there was no way to avoid Mother when you were upset. It was like she had a sixth sense for it.

"I don't need a pep-talk Mother," I said as I took my seat.

"Can't a mother have breakfast with her daughter?" Mother

asked innocently.

I gave her a flat look. "I know how this goes. Someone, usually me, upsets Father so you swoop in and fix everything."

"I'm on your side this time, Feyre," she said. "If I were in your shoes, I would have done the same thing."

"This isn't some sort of trick, is it?" I asked suspiciously.

Mother rolled her eyes, "For Goddesses' sake, Feyre. It's like you forget I'm from Felluna sometimes. Plants and nature are my passions, so yes. I would have done the exact same thing."

I shrugged. "You try to stay neutral normally."

"Dorioya trees are difficult to get past the sapling stage, so losing one as old as the one at the academy simply wouldn't be right."

Leave it to Mother to always make me feel better.

Our conversation ended as two women came with our breakfast. We fell into comfortable small talk as we dug into our pancakes. Once we both finished eating, we remained seated. Mother was finishing her coffee while I sipped on my orange juice. Despite Mother's best effort, I couldn't understand the appeal of coffee. Even if I dumped a pound of sugar into it, I couldn't get past its bitter bite.

I finished my glass first and stood, preparing to say my farewells. Merindah burst into the dining room with wide eyes, stealing my attention. She breathlessly searched the room until her eyes landed on Mother and she ran over.

"What's going on, Merindah?" Mother asked, concerned.

"I was going through the mail today like I always do, and… and…" She held out a letter to Mother. "It's from the Elders."

Not hesitating, Mother took the envelope out of her hand and ripped it open. Her eyes darted over the page as Merindah and I watched, trying to gauge her emotions.

5.

"They've agreed to help," Mother breathed. She then looked up and said it louder, "They've agreed to help!"

The three of us had a brief moment of celebration before Mother grew serious, falling into her Queenly facade.

"Feyre, I need you to get a letter to your father and Council members immediately. Tell them to gather in the War Room. I want you to join them down there."

"Are you sure?" I asked.

"Aren't you the one always begging to be allowed to be involved in meetings?" she asked in return.

"I mean yeah, but I don't think Father would be too happy about me being there."

"And I don't care. He's the one who's been inviting you to meetings lately, so I won't be letting him keep you out of this one," she snipped. With a grin, she added, "Plus, I can't be there because it's Council members only. I need a spy."

Laughing a little, Merindah handed me the small notebook and pen she always kept tucked away in her pocket. I tore a handful of pages out and handed it back. I wrote a quick message simply saying 'Elders agreed to help, meet in the War Room NOW!' then folded them into small squares. I created a handful of aether birds, instructing each one where to go as I handed them a note.

I hurriedly gave Mother and Merindah a quick hug before rushing down to the War Room. As I was getting myself more comfortable, one by one everyone portaled in. Father and Csilla were the first to arrive. Then Amara and Demir. Finally, it was Morana and Drystan.

"The Elders agreed?" Demir asked once everyone was seated. I tossed the letter to the center of the table. "They have."

Father was the first to reach the letter and began reading

41

over it.

"Where do we go from here?" Amara asked.

"They want to have a meeting so we can present them with the evidence we've collected," Father replied.

He then tossed the letter back onto the table where Morana was the next to grab it.

"Does it say when the meeting will be?" Demir asked.

"In three days," Morana answered.

"Drystan, Feyre. I'd like you both to accompany us to the meeting. I think it would be an excellent learning opportunity for you both," Father said.

"Typically, we'd all have to twist your arm to allow them to be involved," Morana retorted.

"They've been part of the last few Council meetings, so it only seems fair to let them tag along," Father replied coolly. "Though there will be one rule. Neither of you will interject. You will watch, listen, and learn what you can from the interaction."

Drystan and I shared a look.

"Thank you, Father," I replied.

"Thank you, King Zander," Drystan said, then looked over to Morana.

We were going to meet the Elders.

6.

Tomorrow was the day we'd be meeting the Elders. Everyone was on edge. Father had spent the day locked away in the War Room with Council going over all the evidence so they could answer any questions the Elders might ask. This meant my usual Wednesday training with Father had to be canceled. After much begging, I managed to rope Alliard into training with me.

"I don't want to hurt you," Alliard nervously said.

I rolled my eyes. "Typically, I'm going against my father. Trust me when I say that you can't do any more damage than he has."

Father and I sometimes went overboard when sparring. He's broken my nose, I've broken a few of his fingers. We always walked out covered in bruises and cuts. It results in Mother giving us the same lecture every week as she tends to our wounds. Sometimes she even mumbles about how we never listened or learned. When Mother mumbled not-so-nice things under her breath, we knew we'd taken things too far.

"But I'm not—"

I threw an aether knife at him. Just before it could hit him, he threw up a wind-shield, deflected it.

"What the—"

I offered no explanation. I threw another blade at him. This time, he deflected the knife and used his wind to put me back a couple of inches. I could see he was no longer anxious when our eyes met. He looked determined.

Keeping my eyes locked with his, I formed an aether sword in each hand. He followed suit by slipping his sword out of its sheath and getting into a fighting stance. I assumed the gears had to be turning in his head right now, trying to guess what my next move would be. I rushed him, swinging both of my swords.

With another strong gust, he shoved me to the side, but I was still able to nick his neck. I quickly regained my balance and rushed him again. He managed to block one of my swords but I halted the other at his thigh.

"This duel-wielding thing doesn't seem very fair," Alliard complained as he pushed me back.

I was still close enough to him that I got another swing in, but he blocked both my swords with his wind-shield.

"And that whole wind thing doesn't seem very fair either," I retorted.

He knocked my legs out from under me, dropping me onto the mat. I twisted so I landed on my back and as I swung my swords upward, they were blocked with his wind. He pointed the tip of his sword at my throat. Agitation bubbled up in my chest as he gave me a small smirk.

"You aren't using your aether enough," he said, holding his hand out to me. "You've got pure, raw magic energy running through your body. You could do a lot of damage with that."

I grabbed his hand, allowing him to pull me to my feet, "I doubt it would be as powerful as you think."

My trainers always taught me that my best bet was to

craft with it. That's why weapons and creatures became my specialties. I'd never tried using it in its raw state against another person.

"Just try," he said with my hand still in his.

I allowed a small amount of aether to slip into Alliard's hand. He winced, withdrawing his touch. It left a minor burn on his palm.

"Now imagine what you could do with that if you were really trying to hurt someone," he said, smiling.

"I don't know..." I said.

"Look, I know you're a good fighter with your swords based on what King Zander has said. But if you're ever in a pinch and need to act quickly, that could be the difference between life and death."

Before I could respond, the training room door cracked open. Alliard and I glanced at one another then took a gigantic step away from each other, creating distance. Mother peeked her head in, searching the room until her eyes settled on us.

"Alliard, I didn't know you were training with her today," she greeted, smiling. "I assumed she was in here whacking away at one of those dummies."

"She asked me to train with her," he replied lamely.

"Do either of you need healing?"

I shook my head. "I went easy on him. Don't want him to get too insecure when he realizes I'm a better fighter."

"Good. I don't need you breaking one of your father's best guards."

"But I can break Father?"

"He helped train you to fight, so I consider it karma," she said, shrugging. "Now, I was coming to get Feyre for dinner, but since you're here too Alliard, I insist you join us."

"Oh, I wouldn't—"

"Tut, tut. Don't think you can start arguing with your Queen now."

I knew she was teasing, but Alliard didn't seem to realize it. Fear flashed in his eyes, though Mother seemed oblivious.

"I'll see you both in the dining room," Mother called over her shoulder as she spun on her heel and left us.

"Don't look so freaked," I said, trying to not laugh.

"I've just never been asked to dine with *royalty* before," he replied.

"Mother and Father see the palace staff and guards as family. *Especially* their personal guards. This won't be the last time this happens, so I'd suggest you get used to it now."

Alliard opened and closed his mouth a few times before simply nodding in response. We made our way to the nearest bathroom to clean ourselves up, then made our way to the dining room.

We were treated to mine and my mother's favorite meal — pancakes with dorioya berries on top. Father was far from the biggest fan, so we only indulged when he wasn't joining us for dinner.

"Thank you for letting me join you for dinner, Queen Calla," Alliard said as he anxiously sat next to me.

"Thank you for joining us," Mother said, smiling. She then turned her attention to me, "I heard your father is letting you and Drystan accompany the Council to the Elders meeting tomorrow."

"I'm not too keen on Drystan being there, but if it means I'll get to continue to stay in the loop with this, then I'll deal with it."

"Who is Drystan?" Alliard asked.

6.

"Morana's heir," I answered.

"And someone who's been chasing after Feyre since he was elected to be Morana's heir," Mother teased.

I rolled my eyes, cutting angrily into my pancakes. "I plan on ruling my own Kingdom, but like most guys, he has a problem accepting 'no' as an answer."

Looking at Alliard, I saw something flash through his eyes. Before I could decipher it, it was gone.

"What do you mean elected?" he asked.

"Moroluma doesn't pass its Kingdom down to the King or Queen's child. Instead, they set up a series of trials that are open to anyone regardless of status. In the end, they give the title of heir to whoever has proved themselves worthy," Mother replied.

"Only the strong can rule a place like Moroluma. At least, that's what they say," I added.

"Things can get chaotic over there. I think it's because the land amplifies people's powers, but who really knows," Mother said with a shrug. "Now, enough of the serious talks. Alliard, why not tell me a bit more about yourself?"

Alliard choked on the water he was drinking, sending him into a coughing fit. "Me?"

Mother giggled. "Yes, you."

He finished clearing his throat. "Um. There isn't much to tell, really. My childhood was pretty normal, I guess. I have a pretty big family. Lots of brothers, sisters, and cousins so there was never a dull moment around the house, but nothing bad. We all had a lot of fun."

"What made you want to be a guard then?" Mother asked.

"My father, grandfather, great grandfather, and so on were all guards," Alliard replied pridefully. "Growing up, they told us stories about how much fun they had, all the friends they made, and all the weird things they got to see. I liked hearing most about their travels through the Kingdoms and cities—"

The dining room doors were thrown open banging thunderously into the walls. Father stood in the doorway, his eyes wide with shock.

Mother dropped her fork onto her plate and rushed wordlessly to him. Alliard and I exchanged worried glances.

"Dear?" Mother said, resting her hand on Father's shoulder. "What's wrong?"

"Artheas," Father breathed out. "It's under attack."

Mother shook her head, frowning in confusion. "What are you talking about?"

"People…a group…they…stormed Artheas…" Father stammered. He stuttered as if he were a child put on the spot. "They're attacking everyone…they're going after everything…"

Mother's hand covered her mouth as she stumbled back a step. "Oh dear god…"

Alliard and I locked eyes, both shocked and fearful. The air in the dining room grew heavy as realization set in. Artheas, our most ancient and beloved Kingdom, was under attack.

More innocent people were drying. There was more destruction. Worst of all, though, it now felt like this was just the beginning.

7.

Father was the first to regain his composure. He wasted no time getting to work.

"Csilla requested that we send any guards we can to assist in guiding citizens safely into the palace," Father said.

Footsteps could be heard outside the dining room. The clinks of armor gave away that they belonged to guards gearing up for a battle. Mother blinked slowly. I swore I could see the gears begin turning in her head.

"What about the rest of Etrayus? What if somewhere else gets attacked?" Mother asked.

"Moroluma, Dradour, and Felluna are being put on lockdown. We are following suit. Demir and Amara have taken responsibility for contacting the cities and towns to warn them and order them to go on lockdown as well," Father answered.

Mother nodded. "Alright. I'll assist you with gathering the guards. Alliard, take Feyre up to her room. And keep her there."

I wanted to push back. To argue and insist that I could help. Deep down I knew that by protesting, I'd be wasting time and putting Artheas at more risk.

A pit formed in my stomach as I nodded. "Be safe."

"We'll come get you as soon as it's all over," Mother comforted.

Nodding in response, Alliard and I walked side by side up to my bedroom. I did my best to stay positive as anxiety began taking over. My hands started to shake and it got harder to breathe.

All the Kingdoms in Etrayus have powerful armies. If they worked together they'd have no problem taking out the threat. This would all be over soon.

Guards were stationed outside my bedroom, awaiting our arrival. Alliard sent me inside, as he linked in the hallway. No doubt trying to get more information about what was happening. Merindah stood at the center of my room, pacing and biting her fingernails. It was a habit I thought she'd grown out of when I grew out of jumping off the ladders in the library.

I cleared my throat, catching her attention. Her eyes locked with mine and she looked relieved. Merindah walked over pulling me into a hug so tight it hurt, but I squeezed her back. After a moment, she released me. I could see the tears threatening to fall.

"I was told to come help keep an eye on you, but everyone was rushing around gathering armor and weapons. I couldn't get anyone to tell me what was going on!" Her voice was shaking.

"Artheas is under attack," I whispered. "I don't know much past that. Father was in shock when he came to tell us and by the time he pulled himself out of it, he and Mother needed to get to work. There wasn't any time for any explanations."

"So you don't know if it's the same people being the academy attack?" Merindah asked.

"Nothing's confirmed," I replied.

She released a shaky breath and sat down heavily at my vanity. "Who would do something like this? Why would they want to do something like this?"

"Power," Alliard answered as he entered the room. "I mean, power and money are why people do most things, isn't it?"

"On the surface, yes," I agreed. "Though there's always a deeper, more selfish reason when it comes to wars."

"War?" Merindah squeaked. "Do you think that's what's happening here?"

"Why else would someone go after The Academy of Etrayus? And now our more ancient Kingdom? It can't be two random, coincidental attacks."

"If you're right, that means this can only be the beginning, so with all due respect, I hope you're wrong," Alliard said.

The last thing I wanted was to be right, but if I was, it posed a question. How do you win in a war when you don't know who you're up against?

~~~~~~~~~~~~~~~~

After a sleepless night for us all, around six in the morning, there was a knock at my door. Merindah and I were both on our feet as soon as we heard it, but Alliard motioned for us to stay put. Hand on his sword, he made his way over to the door, slowly opening it. I let out a sigh of relief when I saw it was only a guard.

I walked up behind Alliard, peering over his shoulder to get a look at the woman. The dark circles under her eyes told me she, like us, had been up all night.

"King Zander and Queen Calla wish to see Princess Feyre and Alliard in the War Room," she recited.

I looked over my shoulder at Merindah who looked anxious all over again.

"Try to get some sleep. I'll have someone update you when we know more," I told her.

She gave me a small encouraging smile and waved me off. I returned her smile before rushing out with Alliard at my side.

We weaved through the palace running down to the basement. I was slow opening the door to give Alliard and I second to compose ourselves. When the door opened, Council was sitting at the round table, each with steaming cups of coffee or tea in front of them.

"There's still some in the pot over there," Demir said, pointing to a table in the corner.

There were mugs, half a pot of coffee, and a kettle of hot water. There were also muffins, toast, and croissants. I snagged a muffin while Alliard poured himself a cup of coffee before we took our seats at the table.

"I'm assuming things have been taken care of," I said optimistically.

"Not exactly," Csilla sighed. "When the sun began to rise, all the people and whatever those monsters were, vanished through the portals they used to get in."

"Wait, wait. What do you mean monsters?" I asked.

"I didn't have time to tell them about everything," Father grimaced.

A small sigh of aggravation left Csilla. "There were these creatures that came through with the people. I assume based on the markings, they were at the academy attack too, which confirms that the attacks are connected."

"Were you able to capture any of them?" I asked.

She shook her head. "We were not, but we managed to kill a few of them so we have bodies to run tests on. They did quite a bit of damage to Artheas' army. Those they killed or injured, something…odd happened to their bodies."

"What do you mean, odd?" Demir asked, scrunching his

eyebrows together.

"It appears to be some sort of infection or poison. We aren't sure yet. We're running tests as we speak," Csilla answered.

"What about the Elders?" Morana asked.

"They're already assisting. Some are running DNA tests on the creatures, others are healing the survivors," Csilla replied. "Also, Elder Eos would like to meet with us all today."

"She's an aether user," I blurted.

My entire body flushed as I focused on the wrapper that was once around my muffin. Now wasn't the time to get giddy over getting to meet Elder Eos. Especially no after what happened last night.

Csilla smiled slightly. "She is. She's also helping our doctors with healing everyone, but she also knows how important it is to meet with us, too. So, she's decided to take responsibility for that. The other Elders won't be there as they are focusing on helping at the hospital and searching Artheas for fresh evidence."

"Alliard, I would like you to accompany us as well," Father said.

Alliard nodded. "Thank you, King Zander. It would be my honor to join you."

"After the meeting, I would like to take you to the morgue to see the creatures," Csilla said. "Does anyone have any other questions or requests before we go?"

Everyone exchanged quizzical glances, but no one seemed to have any questions. Csilla got to her feet, then with a large sweep of her am, opened a portal on the wall behind her. Her earth magic made it look like the brick wall was cracking open. One by one, everyone walked through until it was only Drystan, Alliard, and I standing in the War room.

Drystan rolled his eyes. "I don't understand why Zander is allowing a lowly guard to follow us around and listen in on our meetings," He then let out a dark laugh. "I mean, for all we know, he could be working with the group behind all of this."

"He's been part of my father's personal guard for almost two years and he's now my personal guard. He has more than earned the right to be part of meetings like these," I snapped.

"None of the Council members are traveling around with a guard," he said, smirking. "Then again, not everyone is as pathetic as you are Feyre."

I could see Alliard growing more irritated, which was exactly what Drystan wanted. Drystan loved attention like Morana. Morana commanded attention from her beauty, grace, and the respect everyone held for her. Drystan only got attention because he begged for it like a child.

"Shall we revisit our academy days and tell Alliard about all the times I kicked your ass in training?" I asked, a vengeful smile on my lips.

Drystan narrowed his eyes but said nothing in response.

"I suggest you run along now and stick to clinging to Morana's skirts like a lost puppy and mind your own business for once in your miserable life."

This time he opened his mouth, but I didn't care to hear anything else he had to say. He only did this when no one else was around because he liked to pretend he can be half the ruler that Morana is. There was no point in letting him continue on. I grabbed Alliard's arm, forcing him through the portal before me, then I followed closely behind. We stepped out into a parlor, where Elder Eos was sitting on a couch. She was wearing simple black robes with her gray hair fastened in a tight bun. I heard Drystan step into the room behind

7.

me followed by the portal closing, but by then Csilla was introducing everyone. I stayed focused on her.

"It's lovely to meet you all," Elder Eos said, setting down her teacup. "Now, I will explain to you all how this is going to work. I will be speaking for the Elders during the course of the investigation. I will also only be choosing one of you to meet with me. It will be up to that person to relay our findings and messages to me. I've learned through the years that this is the most effective way to do something like this so if you can't accept that this is how we do things then you can all leave right now."

"We agree to your terms," Father stated.

"Good," Elder Eos said.

Her eyes then slowly started moving down the line. They drifted over each of us a few times and eventually landed on me.

"You, girl." She pointed to me. "Step up."

8.

I hesitated, unsure of what to do. Surely this was some mistake. I wasn't a Council member nor was I part of the investigation.

"I will not ask you again," Elder Eos stated.

That was enough to get my feet moving. I took two steps forward, separating myself from the group. Anxiety was already flooding my system, silently begging me to step back in line and hope she chose someone else.

A small smile formed on her lips. "You're an aether user as well, yes?"

I nodded. "I am. I'm Princess Feyre of Reidell."

I hoped that once she heard I was only a Princess, she'd tell me to step back in line and she'd pick someone else. Instead, she gave me one last once over and nodded decisively.

"I will speak with you and only you. Your guard will have to stay here."

"Uh…I…"I stammered and cleared my throat. "Yes, ma'am."

"Queen Csilla, is it alright if we go to the room across the hall?" Eos asked.

"Of course," Csilla responded.

"Follow me, Feyre."

I glanced over my shoulder at the group. Everyone looked

as confused as I felt. All except Drystan who was seething. I had to suppress a smile looking at him. I turned my attention back to Elder Eos, who patiently waited at the door for me. I hurried to her side and followed her across the hall. There were a handful of guards standing in the hallway who nodded at us as we slipped into the room across the hall. I looked around and it appeared to just be a guest room. I watched as Elder Eos put up a wall of aether in front of the door.

"It creates a bit of interference, so no one will be able to listen in on our conversation," she explained.

"Huh. I never thought about doing something like that," I said, awestruck.

She smiled slightly. "You learn something new every day."

We sat on the couch in front of the fireplace, angling ourselves so we could look at one another.

"Elder Eos, before we begin, I'd like to know — why did you choose me?"

"Please, call me Eos," she said. "And I don't quite have an answer for you. At least, I don't have one that you'd like. I simply felt that you'd be the best fit for the job."

I scrunched my eyebrows together, confused. "But you do know that I'm not an official Council member or anything, right? I'm just here for some hands-on training."

"I understand that, but my gut feelings are never wrong," Eos stated. "Now, with that information in mind, is it safe to assume that you don't know everything that's in the file that Council sent us?"

"I know the crucial pieces like the claw marks and the dorioya tree, but I know little about the finer details."

Eos nodded. "You aren't missing a lot past that. The bulk of the file goes over the tests they ran on the substance they found in the claw marks, the energy masses, and the victim's bodies. They all came back inconclusive."

"So we really have nothing," I said, deflating.

"Not yet, but that's what we're here to help with. We're going to do whatever we can to help get justice for everyone. Whoever is behind this will not be free for much longer," Eos consoled. "Now, I do have one question for you, and I want you to be completely honest."

"Okay."

"Based on what you know and what you've seen, what do you think is going on here?"

I bit the inside of my cheek, hesitant to share my true thoughts. It was one thing to speculate with Alliard and Merindah, but it was entirely different to do that with an Elder.

Eos, seeing my hesitation, said, "I'm merely trying to see where your head is."

"I think someone is trying to start a war," I said.

"Why would they do that?"

I shrugged. "It could be any number of things. Money. Jealousy. Power. Anger."

"I appreciate your honesty, Feyre and I think you're on the right track," Eos agreed. Now she was smiling. "I can't wait to get to work with you."

"What will happen next?" I asked.

"I'm going to get a plan together with the other Elders. After we talk, I will contact you telling you what our next step will be and we will go from there."

Getting to my feet, I held my hand out for her to shake. "Thank you for trusting me to do this."

Eos shook my hand. "You're going to do great, I know it."

With that, I said my farewell and exited the room. I stopped

8.

in the hallway for a minute to take in everything that just happened. The one Elder I'd looked up to for my entire life chose me to work with her. It felt so surreal.

I composed myself and stepped through the parlor door. The room was uncomfortably silent as all eyes fell on me, hopeful and filled with curiosity.

"She's going to speak with the other Elders and decide where they want to start. Then they will contact me and we'll go from there," I said, fidgeting with my hands.

Everyone looked more than a bit disappointed and I understood why. We were all hoping for a bit more information about where they stood, especially after what happened last night. We needed to be patient. It would all come together in the end.

"Let's take a walk through Artheas," Demir said. "I'd like to get an idea of the damage so we can begin working on repairs."

"Is everyone alright doing that before heading to the morgue?" Csilla asked.

Everyone nodded eagerly and Csilla motioned for us to follow her. She led us downstairs and out of the palace. The palace itself looked relatively normal. The shopping district, we quickly realized, was another matter entirely. The once perfect beige cobblestone sidewalks were now deeply gouged by claw marks. Some of the stones were cracked or missing entirely. Trees, grass, flowers, and shrubbery were all dead. Windows were shattered and the glass was scattered everywhere. Some doors were broken and some bricks were chipped and damaged.

The scene began shifting when we got into the neighborhood. This is where things became more horrific and nightmarish. It wasn't just damaged buildings, roads, and sidewalks. There were blood splatters on walls and blood puddles on the ground where bodies once laid. Some houses were nothing but rubble, others looked as though they had been set on fire. Very few appeared to be untouched.

"All the plants are dead, just like at the academy," Amara whispered.

"Do we know what killed them?" Drystan asked.

Amara shook her head. "We've been running tests as well as searching books but we haven't gotten any definitive answers."

"But you have theories?" he asked.

Amara nodded, "Of course."

"The guards who were injured or killed," Alliard said, "Were the creatures able to penetrate their armor?"

"Guards shouldn't be seen or heard," Drystan muttered.

I shot him a threatening glare.

"They cut through it like butter. There was no resistance and no stopping it," Csilla answered. "That's something I wanted to discuss with you, Demir. We're working on better enchantments to strengthen the armor and I wanted to see what our material options might be."

Demir nodded. "In the next few days, I'll bring over my best blacksmiths and architects so we can discuss everything together."

We continued making our way through the neighborhood. All of it truly looked like it had been a battlefield.

"The main points of the attack were the housing district and the temple. The Elders were still preparing for today's meeting when people followed by the creatures burst in. They were able to disable them and escape the tunnels beneath the temple, which allowed them to get into the palace. They quickly found my husband, and he contacted me about what was happening.

8.

By the time the guards made their way to the housing district... most people were asleep already...they tried..." Csilla's voice cracked as tears formed in her eyes. "We tried..."

Amara was the first to jump in and try to comfort Csilla.

"We know," she whispered. "You did everything you could as quickly as you could."

Everyone stopped, allowing Csilla time to collect herself. My eyes couldn't help but wander. The blood in the streets told the gruesome story of what happened here. There were puddles and splatters. There were even smear marks showing people being dragged out of their homes or down the sidewalk. I noticed scuffle marks in some of the larger puddles. People fought for their lives here.

"How many deaths?" I asked, my voice strained.

"Our last count was a little over two hundred," Csilla murmured.

"There aren't any energy masses here," Morana pointed out.

Csilla shook her head. "There were a few, but we captured those upon the Elders' request. It was mainly the creatures killing and attacking. The people who were here seemed to be ordering them around, so there wasn't much magic involved."

"You said you have a couple bodies of these creatures, yes?" Morana asked.

"We have a few, yes. If you're all satisfied with our walk around, then we can portal to the morgue now," Csilla said, having regained her composure.

"I think I've seen enough," Father said, his voice strained.

"I think we all have," Amara said.

Csilla crafted another portal. Stepping through, we found ourselves in the basement of the hospital outside the morgue. It was cold. The medicinal, sanitary smell of the hospital quickly gifted me a headache. Csilla led us through a pair of double doors into the morgue. From there, we went through a larger door into a larger refrigerated room where four dead creatures lay. They were horrific.

They seemed to be made of pure muscles. Their arms were huge, but their haunches were larger. They couldn't be the fastest creature based on their side, but there was no doubt that they were powerful. Their skin was leathery and smooth. There wasn't a strand of hair anywhere on them that I could see. They didn't have ears either. Only holes where they should be.

My eyes then drifted down to their hands that were hanging off the stretchers. It became very clear how they could make their marks in bricks and stone. One of their claws was as thick as three of my fingers put together. If those were their claws, I wasn't sure I wanted to know what their teeth looked like.

"So. This is what we're up against," Father stated.

"It took a great deal of effort to kill these four. Their skin is like armor, their claws are coated in what we suspect is venom, and their teeth can inject what we assume is the same venom," Csilla said.

"You suspect?" Morana asked.

"We're comparing it to samples we took from their claws and the victims to confirm."

"Do we know anything about this venom?" I asked.

"So far, it doesn't match any known venoms, toxins, or poisons from neither animals nor plants. But, we've barely scratched the surface on samples so we're still running comparisons. We're unsure about how long it will take to get through them all."

8.

These things are completely unknown to us. We had no clue what they were, where they came from, or the best way to kill them. Great, just when I thought they couldn't be any more dangerous.

"I'd like to see some samples of this venom. Maybe I have something in the Enchanted Forest that could help," Amara suggested.

"And I'd like to see these energy masses," Morana stated.

"I can take you all up to a conference room and have someone bring samples of everything if you'd like," Csilla replied.

I shook my head. "If you don't mind, I'd like to skip that."

Drystan didn't bother trying to hide his smugness. Right now, I didn't care. I'd seen enough horrors for one day.

"I'd like to skip too. I need to gather my people so we can begin work on this new armor and gathering materials we need to begin repairs," Demir said.

Father stepped back to where Alliard and I were standing. He pulled me into a quick hug saying, "You did well today." He looked at Alliard and ordered, "Take her home and keep her close. After last night's attack, who knows what's going to happen next."

9.

The portal Alliard created led us to the palace steps. Without hesitation, he started toward the front doors. I didn't. I wasn't ready to get locked away in the palace again just yet. I needed time to process what I'd just seen and clear my mind.

Alliard looked over his shoulder. "Are you coming?"

"Could we go walk around the Kingdom for a bit?" I asked.

He shrugged. "I mean, Reidell's going to be on lockdown for another hour or two, so I don't see why not."

We walked through the palace gates onto the sidewalk. We were silent for what must have been the better half of a half-hour. I stole glances, but he was lost in his own world, oblivious to my searching gaze. A few more minutes passed and Alliard stopped abruptly. He stepped in front of me, forcing me to stop too.

"Can I ask you something?" he asked.

"Sure."

"Are you okay?"

"Do I seem not okay?"

"I don't know. You just didn't seem to be doing too well in Artheas, so I wanted to see if maybe…you wanted to talk about it."

9.

I wanted nothing more than to brush him off and insist that I was alright. Maybe tired from not sleeping. The idea of talking to Alliard about my feelings felt odd. We'd been spending a lot of time together lately — we'd talked about the attack, we joked, we got to know each other. But, he was still my guard first. And my friend second. If we could even be friends, that is.

Talking about it would make me feel better, though...

I sighed, toeing the ground. "I've never had to see that much blood, or body bags, or dead bodies. I've never had to wake up in the morning or go to bed at night being afraid that another Kingdom or town is going to be attacked. I've never had to *deal* with people being outraged at Council. It's just all...overwhelming." I couldn't bring myself to meet his eyes. Saying this out loud was hard enough without looking at him.

"Well, hey. The Elders are assisting us now. And we have the bodies of those creatures! Two big things we didn't have before. For all we know, by the end of the day, we could be ten steps closer to getting justice for everyone and solving this mystery."

"How can you be so calm looking at all of that or talking about that?" I asked, looking up at him.

He shrugged, his face falling. "During training, they put guards through this sort of conditioning class. We're shown the horrors and realities of battle. Dead bodies, blood, serious injuries. More gore than you could imagine. They do it to prepare us so we won't freeze or panic when it matters most."

I shook my head, wrapping my arms around myself. "I don't think I could ever get used to seeing these things."

"It was definitely jarring at first. I was one of many who ran out of the room to throw up our lunch," Alliard admitted.

I laughed despite myself. "Really?"

"Yup," he said, laughing with me. "Not my finest moment, that's for sure."

"I'd hoped that I'd never have to witness any of this in my lifetime. I know it's probably a naive way of thinking, but I guess I was just trying to be optimistic."

"Things like this have rarely happened in Etrayus, so I don't think it's naive to have that hope. I mean, I thought my career was going to be a pretty boring one too. I never in a million years thought I'd be assigned to a Princess to help protect her from some mysterious group or unknown monsters."

A small smile found its way onto my face. I was grateful for his optimism and willingness to open up to me.

Without thinking, I took a step forward and wrapped my arms around his neck, pulling him into a tight hug. He tensed briefly before relaxing and wrapping his arms around my waist.

"Thank you," I whispered. "You've helped me more than you probably realize."

I stepped away from him, forcing him to loosen his hold. We locked eyes and something about the way he looked at me filled my stomach with butterflies. After what felt like a lifetime, Alliard took a step away from me, creating more distance between us, suddenly interested in everything that wasn't me.

He cleared his throat. "We should probably start heading back. I don't want King Zander to get back and we're nowhere to be seen."

"Um. Yeah. Right."

Slowly, we both turned in the direction of the palace and began walking. We filled the whole walk back with an awkward silence neither of us tried to break.

9.

We arrived back at the palace and turned to each other, preparing our goodbyes. Then the realization seemed to strike us both as we stood staring open-mouthed at one another. We couldn't go our separate ways. Father ordered him to stay at my side at all times. There was no avoiding this.

"Where to next?" he asked.

"Um. Up to my bedroom," I said. My cheeks felt like they were on fire.

He nodded and waited for me to lead the way. I walked into the palace and bee-lined it for the stairs, hoping to avoid any familiar faces. When we got up to my room, Alliard gently pushed me to the side so he could step in first. He took a quick look around to make sure things were safe, then motioned me inside.

"I'm going to change. Go ahead and make yourself comfortable," I said.

Not giving him time to respond, I disappeared into my closet, closing and locking the door behind me. I plopped myself on the bench next to where I stored my shoes. Once alone, embarrassment took hold. I hugged him. I thanked him. Then it turned into the most awkward interaction we've ever had. To add insult to injury, there was no avoiding each other. We were stuck together.

"Um. Feyre! There's something out here that I assume is for you!" Alliard shouted.

"I'll be out in a minute!" I shouted back.

I was hoping to have some time to myself, but it didn't seem like luck was on my side today. Boxing away my need to vanish from mortification, I quickly changed out of my dress and into pants and a tunic and slipped back into my room.

An aether bird sat on my vanity.

"It...it phased through the window," Alliard said, staring reverently at it.

"Have you never seen a messenger bird created by magic?" I asked.

"Maybe once or twice, but I don't think I've ever seen one do...that."

I moved toward my vanity. As soon as the bird saw me, it did a little hop and a letter materialized in front of it. I saw my name scrawled elegantly in handwriting I didn't recognize across the front of the envelope. I opened it cautiously. I slipped out the note and skimmed to the bottom to see who had signed it. Elder Eos.

A pit of anxiety formed in my stomach and I deflated a bit. I had expected to have a day or two to warm up to the idea of my new job before I was called in. Once again, luck wasn't on my side today.

I was to meet Eos and the Elders at The Academy of Etrayus tomorrow. She added that my guard could accompany us if needed. I hoped that this awkwardness would pass by then.

I wrote a quick letter back informing her that we'd be there and held it out to the aether bird. It leaned forward, touching the paper with its beak. The paper disappeared, and the bird flew back through the window.

10.

Letting out an aggravated sigh, I slid down to the floor. I was supposed to be getting ready to meet the Elders, but I had no idea what I was supposed to wear. Was I supposed to keep it formal or was I supposed to go more casual?

My parents and Merindah trained me on how to conduct myself during a ball or a meeting. They'd trained me on how to manage and run a whole Kingdom. But I had no idea what I was supposed to wear to something like this.

Mother's voice cut through my thoughts. "You're overthinking it."

"I just want to make a good impression," I said. "Everyone's trust me to do this, and I'd like to show that Elder Eos didn't make a mistake in choosing me."

"Then let's see what I can do to help," Mother said, smiling.

Before I could respond, Mother turned her attention to all my clothes. She picked out a simple teal dress with a fluffy skirt, perfect for the spring weather. She followed that up with a pair of leggings and boots.

"I'd also like for you to wear your cloak," Mother said. "After the Artheas attack, I don't want to take any risks."

"Yes ma'am."

I pushed myself up from the floor, taking the outfit from Mother. She gave me an encouraging smile and left me to get dressed. I slipped into my clothes as quickly as I could, then took a seat at my vanity. I quickly ran a brush through my hair and applied some mascara. I smiled at myself in the mirror when I saw how good I looked. Mother always knew best.

Following a knock at my door, Alliard strolled in.

"Can you pass me my cloak?" I asked him.

"Sure."

He unhooked it from the wall and draped it over my shoulder. A shiver ran down my spine when I felt his breath on my neck. I did my best to ignore it as I clipped my cloak on the throat and turned to face him. He was closer than I thought he was.

I looked up at him with wide eyes. "Are…are you ready?"

"As I'll ever be," he said.

I created the portal, and he stepped through it first. I followed closely behind. We appeared, once again, by the administrative building. Merely a few seconds later, a portal formed in front of us, and out stepped Elder Eos.

Just Elder Eos.

"Feyre, you look lovely," Eos said, smiling. "I really appreciate you taking time out of your day for this."

"It's no big deal, really. I want this all to come to an end as much as everyone else. I'll help out in any way that I can," I replied. "Where are the other Elders? I thought they were joining us."

"We decided it would be best if they stayed in Artheas to assist Queen Csilla in the hospital and labs. I believe people from Dradour are beginning the repairs today too," she answered. "We've determined that those creatures do indeed have some sort of venom coating their claws and in their saliva, but we aren't sure exactly what it is. The infected are only getting worse, but Amara and creating antibiotics based on what little information we do have. We're hoping they'll at least buy us some time."

"You haven't been able to heal them using magic?" Alliard asked.

"You must be Feyre's guard. I apologize, I don't remember your name," Eos said. "But no, we haven't been able to heal them using magic. They tried that with the first few infected when they arrived at the hospital, but they began rotting from the inside out and died before we realized what was happening. We have to find a way to eradicate the toxin entirely before we can heal them."

Alliard bowed slightly and said, "I'm Alliard.

"It's lovely to meet you, Alliard. I only wish it was under better circumstances," Eos said, smiling.

"If you can't heal their wounds, then how can you keep them alive?" I asked.

"They stitched them up enough that bleeding out isn't a concern and we have put them into sterile rooms in hopes of keeping away any infections. Their wounds are being cleaned regularly. It isn't ideal, but it's all that can be done right now."

"Well, I guess we should get started with our exploration, then. Maybe you'll see something that will help point you all in the right direction," I said optimistically.

"Have you seen the campus at all?" Eos asked.

"I've been through about half of it. I stopped at the courtyard where the dorioya tree is."

She nodded as we fell into step side by side. Alliard hung back a few strides doing his best to make himself invisible.

Our first stop was the claw marks. Eos looked at them long

enough to take a few swabs of them before continuing on.

"There's residue of the venom here. I'd like to have as many samples of it as possible so we can easily link the attacks together for a trial," Eos said.

She sealed away the swabs in a glass tube, putting them away in her bag. We carried on stopping every few minutes so Eos could take a sample of what seemed like everything. Dead grass, energy masses, the dirt, more swabs from claw marks, and everything in between. While she took samples and made notes of them in her notebook, she explained their relevancy.

Things carried on this way until we got to the courtyard where the dorioya tree lived. I was over the moon to see it alive and glowing brightly. Energy masses were still floating around it, but they didn't seem to be attacking it anymore. Maybe they'd learned their lesson.

"There are a lot of energies here on campus," Eos said. "I was hoping I'd be able to hone in on one or two powerful energies to match them to a suspect, but there's far too many. It was the same way in Artheas."

"So, we've got nothing," I said flatly.

It was getting harder and harder to control my frustration with it all. I just wanted something, even if it was something minuscule, to tell us we were getting closer to putting an end to this.

"Don't be so pessimistic, Feyre. I'll take as many as I can back with me and run tests on them. Maybe we'll be able to find some similarities."

"And if we can't find any?" I asked.

"Then we focus on the creatures and their venom," Eos answered smoothly. "Someone created them from the ground up. That requires knowledge, time, and experimentation. They can't do all of that without leaving some sort of trace behind."

I scrunched my eyebrows together. "What do you mean someone created them from the ground up?"

"Amara and Morana have been looking over every book in Etrayus as well as interviewing some summoners on their teams and these creatures are not known to anyone. They aren't summoned from the afterlife or the underworld or another realm. They're living, breathing creatures that someone had to have created," Eos explained.

"I didn't know it was possible," I said.

"It isn't an easy thing to do, but if you have the determination and dedication, it is possible."

Without another word, Eos began walking around stuffing energy masses into glass tubes. This left me alone with my thoughts.

If someone created these things then that had to narrow down the suspect pool by magic alone. I knew divine users like myself couldn't create life like that. My aether birds lasted long enough to do their task and then they dissipated, their energy either returning to my body or the air. What sort of process and experiments did it take to create something like these creatures?

I snapped myself out of my head. I needed to focus on what was happening here in front of me. There would be time for speculation later.

"You might want to swab the dorioya tree, too," I suggested.

"The file mentioned that the tree had been attacked and you tried to heal it."

"It's glowing again and the energy coming from it is strong. It wasn't like the night that I healed it. Alliard can attest to that."

"It was dull and weak," Alliard agreed.

Eos made her way over to the tree to take samples. She started with swabs, then took cuttings of where the tree had been cut.

"You healed it with you aether, yes?"

"Of course."

"Hmm."

Alliard and I glanced at each other, seeming to have the same train of thought.

"Have you not tried aether on the victims?" Alliard asked before I could.

Eos shook her head. "I wanted to try, but the doctors decided that it would be a bad idea. If life magic and healing magic couldn't do anything, then why would aether be able to do anything different? I tried pushing back, but their answer was ultimately no."

"Aether and light are a lot different from life and healing, Everyone knows that," I said, feeling slightly offended.

"Everyone does, but they weren't willing to risk any more lives to let me try," Eos sighed. "While I'm upset and think that you're right, I don't want to risk anyone's life either."

Wordlessly, we continued on our way through the rest of the campus. The back half of the campus was staff housing, the farm, and the training grounds. The staff building was nothing but a pile of bricks, like the two dormitory buildings. Everything on the farm was dead. The training grounds, however, seemed untouched. All the targets were still standing. The small building that held practice weapons was still erect. The grass here was even still alive.

"It seems they made it to this point and just stopped," Alliard commented.

10.

I shrugged. "It's just the training grounds. Why would they bother destroying everything here?"

Eos walked ahead of us, pausing when she got to the space we dubbed the arena. It was a large circle of sand we used for sparring.

"This is where they entered," Eos said. She seemed to be talking to herself.

Alliard and I quickly made our way over and sure enough, there were who knows how many footprints in the sand. Some were shoe prints, but there were tracks that certainly weren't human overlapping them. Those had to be from the creatures.

"After they shattered the wards and took out the perimeter guards, the bulk of them entered here at the very edge of the campus and made their way to where they knew everyone would be," Eos explained.

Alliard pushed air out of his nose. "No wonder no one spotted them. The guards don't patrol all the way out here."

"So they came from the back. Killed everyone in the staff buildings and the guards there. Then made their way through the rest of the campus, killing who they saw and destroying the buildings," Eos mumbled.

"It's genius," I said. "Anyone who could stop them, like the teachers or guards, would have already been killed or at the very least disabled. With all the chaos, any guards who survived would start trying to set off the alarms and alert people. That left them distracted and more open to attacks."

"They had to know exactly what they were doing in order to pull that off," Alliard pointed out. "Protocols, guard paths, the campus layout, how to disable the alarms. The guards frequently change things to avoid this exact thing, though."

"So many questions and no answers," I mumbled.

Eos spoke," Feyre, I know you're worried but—"

I cut her off. "Everyone's expecting the Elders and your ancient knowledge to swoop in and solve the case. Everyone's expecting you to know exactly what to do to get the answers we need! In reality, you're just as clueless and hopeless as the rest of us."

"We're trying our best, Feyre. We're all doing what we can with the knowledge we have to end this swiftly and easily." Her voice came out strained as if she were holding back.

"And I understand that. But that might not be good enough!" I snapped, exasperated.

Eos opened her mouth, but nothing came out. She slowly pressed her lips together, looking as defeated as I felt. After a minute or two, she seemed to collect herself. A look of determination settled on her face.

"We're going to get justice for everyone who has been affected by this," she said firmly. "Tell Council about everything we discussed here today. I'll send another letter when it's time to meet again."

I opened my mouth to say something, or maybe apologize. Before I could, Eos had disappeared through a portal, leaving Alliard and I alone.

11.

I was sitting in my parents' office silently listening to them discuss everything I'd found out from Eos. They were trying to figure out where to go from here while acting like I wasn't in the room. I tried to speak up or share my opinions, but I got cut off and ignored. After the third or fourth time, my agitation rose to the surface.

"If you're going to just talk over me, then why am I here?" I shouted over them.

"I'm sorry," Mother sighed. "We're just trying to process all of this."

"I want to speak to Council first. Amara, Csilla, and Morana can give us more insight since they're working alongside the Elders," Father said.

"This is all something I need to be part of. If Elder Eos sends me another letter tonight, then I'd like to show up with something to report even if it's something small," I said.

They grew quiet for a moment, exchanging a look. Then they sighed in unison.

"If you don't mind, I'd like to keep you and Drystan out of this meeting. I want updates from everyone. Having extra voices asking questions and offering opinions might make things more confusing," Father stated.

I bit the inside of my cheek to keep from saying something I'd regret. He was still my father so I had to have some level of respect for him, but I wanted nothing more than to rip his head off. I wanted to be at that meeting. I needed to be there.

"Then I'd like to go out of town this weekend," I stated.

"Feyre—"

"I need a break from all of this," I said. "I need a break from people dying and being attacked and I'm tired of having to have conversations where everyone says we have no new information. I'm tired of it."

Mother laid her hand on Father's shoulder silencing him before he could speak again. "She's more than earned a weekend away from all of this, Zander. Especially if you don't need her this weekend."

"It's too risky for her to wander off right now. Artheas was just attacked!" Father argued.

"She'll have Alliard with her."

"I don't care."

"You can't want to protect her from the world one second and let her be independent the next!"

Another heated conversation ensued between them. This time, I didn't try interjecting myself into their bickering. I sat back, knowing that Mother would be able to convince him. All I had to do was let her work her magic.

"Alright! Alright!" Father finally growled. "She can go!" He then turned to me. "You take Alliard with you and you do not leave his side. If he gets a weird feeling and wants to leave, you listen to him. Do I make myself clear?"

"Crystal."

"Where are you planning on going?" he asked.

I shrugged. "Not a clue. I'll let the wind guide me."

11.

Father wasn't too pleased with my answer, but before he could try to argue I was up and walking out.

"Be careful! And take your cloak with you!" Mother shouted as I walked out of the office.

I made my way up to my bedroom to pack a bag and switched my flats out for boots. I folded my cloak and put it on top of everything so I wouldn't have to search for it later. When I finished, I swung my bag over my shoulder and made my way to the male barracks so I could snag Alliard. On the way over, I stopped a staff member instructing them to get a coach prepared for me.

As I approached the barracks, I could hear the guards laughing, joking, and chatting away. Until the door closed behind me. All eyes quickly found me and the once relaxed air turned tense and awkward. They exchanged glances, unsure of what to do.

"I'm not here with more horrible news or to send you into another battle. I'm just looking for Alliard," I said.

They all seemed to visibly relax a bit and returned their attention to their earlier conversations. I caught a few of the newer guards checking me out before their eyes darted away.

"Alliard! Common room!" someone shouted.

A minute later Alliard stepped out of a room wearing only a towel around his waist and water dripping down his body. I couldn't stop my eyes from following the water droplets that were sliding down his torso. He was more muscular than I expected him to be. I quickly focused back on his eyes hoping that I hadn't been too obvious.

"Feyre, what are you doing here?" he asked, his cheeks turning red.

"We've got the weekend off, so pack a bag," I said.

He shifted his weight slightly between his feet, gripping his towel tightly. "Is this a pre-approved trip or…?"

"It wasn't easy, but it's pre-approved." I grinned. "There will be a coach waiting at the palace steps, don't take too long."

Not waiting for a response, I turned on my heel and made my way out of the barracks. I took my time getting to the front of the palace. When I arrived, the coach was ready. The coachman opened the door for me and I slipped inside, setting my bag on the bench next to me.

I wasn't sure how much time had passed when Alliard finally made an appearance, but he eventually took a spot on the bench across from me. He dressed a bit more casually, telling me he was taking this mini-vacation seriously. I couldn't help but notice that his shirt was tighter than anything I'd seen him in before, making his muscles more noticeable. I tried to not stare too much.

"Where are we headed?" he asked as the coach started moving.

"Khisfire," I answered.

Alliard's eyes grew wide. "Isn't that where criminals and mercenaries meet up to make deals and network together?"

"They like to stay there, but they're good people."

"So you've been there before?"

I shrugged. "It's a place I go to when I need to get away. I have a bit of an understanding with everyone there. They respect me, but they don't treat me like royalty and watch my back in case anyone they aren't familiar with rolls into town."

Eyeing me, he asked, "What sort of understanding?"

"I work with a few of the more important people in town. We exchange information but sometimes I hire them to get information for me," I answered.

11.

"So we're going there for a reason."

"I'm hoping to meet with a friend of mine named Dughall. He's a bounty hunter and informant. I want to know what's going on in the rest of Etrayus and what rumors are surrounding the academy attack."

Calling Dughall a friend was a bit of an understatement. Things between us sometimes were a bit more than friendly, but that wasn't something Alliard needed to know.

"What am I supposed to tell people who ask what we did?" Alliard asked.

"We went to some high-end tourist town, stayed in the best hotel suite, hung out eating expensive food, and you accompanied me on a shopping spree," I answered.

He smirked. "So, I got a vacation on your parents' dime but also got stuck carrying your shopping bags. I think I can work with that."

"I mean, it's technically true. We just aren't going to a high-end tourist town and staying in a glamorous suite."

He smiled. "That just means you owe me a high-end vacation."

"I think I can make that happen when all this madness is over."

~~~~~~~~~~~~~~~

Four hours later, we arrived in Khisfire. The coachman dropped us off in front of the Inn before turning back to take the horses to the stable and get himself a room for the night. Alliard grabbed my bag for me and I led us into the Inn.

The girl behind the counter let out an excited shriek as she saw us. Before I knew it, I was being pulled into a tight hug while a tense Alliard stood off to the side.

"I was wondering when you'd be gracing us with our presence again!" she squealed, letting go.

"With everything going on, it's been hard to get out of the palace, let alone Reidell," I said.

"I should've assumed your parents were keeping you on lockdown with all these nasty attacks."

"It's not all bad. They've been letting me in on some of the meetings and important, top-secret stuff."

"Our Princess is moving up in the world," She grinned. I watched her eyes drift over to Alliard, who hadn't moved. "Who's this handsome man?"

"This is Alliard, my personal guard, until further notice," I answered. "Alliard, this is Rin. Her family has owned this inn for too long to say honestly."

Alliard nodded. "It's nice to meet you."

"Oh trust me, the honor is all mine," Rin said. She didn't bother trying to hide her eyes exploring his body. "Are all your guards this attractive?"

"Definitely not," I admitted.

"Well, even you having this one is enough to make me jealous," she said grinning. "Now. I'll assume that we're going to be giving Alliard here the same treatment we give you."

We made our way over to the counter so Rin could get us checked in.

"You assumed correctly," I said, laughing softly. "So, if he gets too rowdy or wasted they're more than welcome to drag him out of the bar kicking and screaming."

"I'll be sure to let everyone know," Rin laughed with me. "Would you like your usual room, or would you prefer one with two beds?"

"Two beds, please."

"You're going to torture the poor guy, got it," she said, writing

11.

something down. A second later, she dropped a key onto the counter and slid it over to me. "Room twelve is all yours. It's on the second floor."

"Thank you."

Alliard and I were able to find our room quickly. I unlocked the door and pushed it open, revealing a simple but comfortable room. Dark hardwood floors, blue-gray walls, and a couch in front of a fireplace. The bathroom was off to the left and the beds had perfect, crisp white linens on them.

"We don't really have much to do until the sun sets. Nothing fun happens around here until nightfall," I said.

"Aren't you too young to have any sort of real fun?" Alliard asked.

I rolled my eyes. "They bend the rules a little for me. They get plenty of money from me, so there's no reason for them to not let me have my fun."

Alliard set his bag on one bed and mine on the other. He seemed to go into guard mode after that as he locked the door and made sure the windows were locked too. I, on the other hand, kicked my boots off and got comfortable on my bed.

"I'm going to take a little nap so I can survive the night. I suggest you try to do the same."

Alliard stiffly sat on the edge of his bed while I slipped beneath my sheets. I knew he'd struggle to sleep in an unfamiliar place, but I hoped that he'd at least try.

12.

My eyes opened to a pitch-black room. I'd overslept, but I wasn't too worried about it. It only meant that everyone was sure to be there already, so the fun would be in full swing.

I turned a lamp on and searched the room until I spotted Alliard. He was fast asleep on the couch, sitting up with his head slumped over its back. He looked calm and peaceful, which was a bit of an odd sight. Even if he appeared cool and collected, he had an intensity in his eyes that lent to his intimidating appearance. He took his job as a guard seriously at all times. It's part of why Father liked him so much. It's why I trusted him so much.

I pulled myself out of bed and padded over to the couch. I gently touched his shoulder. Alliard jolted awake, his eyes were wide as he reached for his sword.

"It's me!" I shouted. "It's just me!"

He froze as his brain processed his surroundings. Then he relaxed.

"Sorry," he said.

"Are you ready to get going?" I asked.

"Where?"

I grinned. "A bar. Where criminals like to hang out."

12.

He groaned. "Please tell me you're kidding."

"Of course I am," I replied. "They're not all criminals."

"I'm starting to regret agreeing to this," he said as he got to his feet.

"They're harmless. They're just mercenaries, private investigators, and thieves trying to make a living."

He rolled his eyes but stuffed his feet into his shoes without further complaint. I got my boots on and ran my fingers through my hair to make it look less like I'd just woken up. Excitement bubbled up inside me at the thought of being able to let loose for a night.

Alliard took a couple of daggers out of his bag, then strapped his sword to his back.

Eyeing his sword, I said, "You don't have to be that worried."

"We're going to be surrounded by people, most of whom I'm sure you don't know. So. There's many reasons to be this worried."

"Nothing's going to happen," I said, rolling my eyes.

Alliard stared directly into my eyes. "Feyre, I'm your guard. I'm going to be ready to protect you, no matter what."

My cheeks grew flushed, but I refused to look away. "Fine. Let's get going."

We made our way out of the inn, stopping to say goodbye to Rin for the night. The bar was right up the roach, so it didn't take long to get there. We stepped inside the stone building where the festivities were already in full swing. It was packed, which was enough to get Alliard to tense up.

I linked my arm through his, giving him no other choice but to walk with me through the crowd. I took him over to the bar, stopping here and there to introduce him to some friends of mine. Everyone walked him with open arms. There were even a few ladies who were already eyeballing him. A pang of jealousy surfaced, but I quickly suppressed it before it could rear its ugly head.

We snagged a couple of seats at the end of the bar. The bartender quickly slid beers and menus in front of us. Alliard's eyes were darting around the room, taking everything and everyone in as I sipped my beer and flipped through the menu.

"No one's stupid enough to try anything in here, Alliard. Try to relax a little."

He let out a small sigh. "Fine, but I'm not drinking." He was already waving down the bartender as he spoke. "Can I have water instead?"

The bartender took the beer away and replaced it with a glass of water soon after, leaving me to drink alone. We opted for hamburgers and fries. After we ordered, he fell into comfortable small talk as he asked me about some of the people I'd introduced him to. It didn't take us long to get interrupted by Dughall, though.

It was hard to ignore how attractive he was. His golden hair, beard, and amber eyes were enough to make any girl swoon. He was tall, muscular, and loved to sweet-talk anyone with a pretty face. It was his flirting and dedication to his work that made it impossible for him to get a girl who was truly deserving of him. That didn't stop people like me from using him to blow off a bit of steam or get showered with affection for a couple of nights.

"Feyre! Lovely to see you again!" He smiled.

"Dughall. I wasn't expecting you to be here so early in the night."

"I'll admit, I'm supposed to be meeting with some people, but I heard you got here and I know you wanted to talk so I had to grace you with my presence first," he said. "But I have a question for you first."

I rolled my eyes as a smile found its way to my face. "What do you want?"

"Is it true that Artheas was attacked?"

I quickly schooled my expression, allowing myself to become emotionless. Council and the Elders had done what they could to keep the news of the attack from getting out to the public. The academy attack had caused enough fear and upset that we were still dealing with. If everyone found out that Artheas had been attacked too, things would become worse. They had manufactured a story that Artheas was closed so basic repairs and maintenance could be done. I'm sure no one believed it, but no one had the evidence to argue that something more sinister was going on.

"People really need to stop coming up with these wild stories," I grumbled.

Dughall grew serious. "Don't play dumb with me Feyre."

"Then don't act stupid, Dughall," I said, following his lead. "You know our deal and right now you aren't holding up your end of it. Give me something worthwhile or drop it."

Dughall smirked. "Lose the guard dog and I'll give you plenty."

"I suggest you get lost before I make you swallow your teeth," Alliard snapped.

"Oh? He speaks?" Dughall said, pretending to get excited. "What other tricks does he do?"

"Don't be an ass," I said. "Either give me something or drop it."

"Alright, alright. I do have something for you."

"Then spit it out."

His eyes darted over to Alliard. "Can he be trusted?"

"He wouldn't be here if I didn't trust him. You know that," I said.

"Word on the street is that some powerful royal is out there spending millions hiring any and all criminals they can find," Dughall said.

"I'm going to need something more than that if you want answers for the questions you're asking."

"It's that guy from Moroluma. The creepy one with the silver hair and black eyes, super skinny."

I raised an eyebrow. "Drystan?"

"Him! Yeah. He's pretty hard to mistake for anyone else."

"Alliard, do me a favor and ask around to confirm his story. Stick to the people I introduced you to," I ordered.

He glanced at Dughall but hesitantly did as I asked. I watched him make his way through the crowd. Every few seconds he glanced my way, never giving someone all of his attention.

"Come on Fey. Have I ever lied to you?" Dughall asked.

"No, but you're making a pretty big claim and if it's true, I'll need you to get more information for me."

I didn't believe that Drystan could be doing anything shady. Especially not since he's always glued to Morana's hip. However, he did have friends in low places because of his past. They'd have no problem impersonating him with illusion magic and if that's what was happening, I wanted to know.

"So the Princess needs a lowly criminal's help. What's in it for me?"

"Get me concrete proof about what's happening and I'll get you whatever you want like usual."

I refused to say anything more. I sat back, watching Alliard make his way around the room. It took a while, but eventually,

12.

Alliard finished his rounds and made his way back over to us.

"They seem to have all heard the same thing. He's apparently offering about fifty thousand to anyone willing to help, but he won't give anyone any details about what he needs help with, so people are hesitant about reaching out to him," Alliard said.

I shrugged and said, "Good enough for me."

Before I could say anything more, Alliard stopped me. "Are you sure you can trust him with this? Are you sure you can trust anyone here?"

"Dughall's been nothing but loyal to me and has kept every secret I've ever told him since the day we met. As for everyone else, they wouldn't lie about something this big."

"More importantly, they wouldn't lie to me. My family practically runs this town so no one would risk getting on our bad sides," Dughall said. He met Alliard's eyes for the first time tonight. "And as for Feyre, I've bent and broken a lot of rules for Feyre to give her information. I'd never do anything to put her in harm's way and I'd certainly never lie to her or betray her."

Alliard held his gaze for what felt like an eternity before looking over at me, giving me a nod of approval. So, I led them to a back room, put up a wall of aether for interference, and I told Dughall about Artheas. I even told him about the Elders, the poisoned victims, and the creatures. All things no one knew except those within Council and their tight circle.

"I'll see what else I can find out about Drystan and see what he's up to," Dughall said. "Do you think he could have anything to do with the attacks?"

It shocked me a little to hear Dughall ask if he could be behind the attacks. Drystan wasn't the nicest person and he wanted power more than anything, but he wouldn't stoop this low. Not when he'd already secured his spot as an heir. He had what he wanted, so there would be no need for this.

"Of course not. I'm not even entirely convinced that this is really Drystan hiring people," I said. "That being said, I don't trust him and if he is up to something shady, I'd like to know what it is."

"If I can find anything, I'll reach out," Dughall said. "I should get to that meeting now, though. It was nice seeing you again Fey, and it was an honor getting to meet your guard dog."

Before Alliard could snarl a threat out, Dughall left the room disappearing into the crowd. It was almost as if he were never even here.

"I hope he's as *wonderful* and trustworthy as you think he is," Alliard sighed.

"If he wasn't, I wouldn't have said anything," I replied. I dropped my serious exterior replacing it with a small smile. "Now enough business. We need to get back to our vacation."

We went back out to the bar where I chugged the rest of my beer and our food was waiting. I motioned the bartender to bring me another. Alliard smiled, shaking his head as he started eating.

13.

Alliard and I were at the bar until two in the morning. There weren't many people who stuck around that long. Even with a small group, we managed to have fun. Alliard, who had been very tense and uptight in the beginning, ended up being the life of the party even while being stone-cold sober. He cut me off after two beers. In the moment, I felt upset, but now I was glad he did. For what felt like the first time, I wasn't stumbling through the streets of Khisfire, needing someone's help to get back to the inn. All in all, it had easily been the best night I'd had in a while.

We were about halfway between the bar and the inn when Alliard stopped suddenly. He frantically began looking around, searching for something.

"What's up?" I asked.

"Something in the air shifted," he said, continuing to look around.

That was enough to put me on edge. I trusted Alliard's instincts. If he thought something was off, then something was, more than likely, off. I formed a handful of aether orbs and scattered them around us so we could see better. The lanterns in Khisfire were old and dim making it difficult to get around at night.

With the area lit up, I expected to see something. There was nothing. Only us.

"Maybe you're just on edge because you're in an unfamiliar place," I suggested. I hoped that was the case.

"No. There's something out there," Alliard insisted.

"How do you know?"

He shook his head. "I don't know how to explain it. The air is…tainted in a way. It's not clean and clear."

I realized I didn't know much about Alliard's powers. I knew he could create shields, manipulate the wind, and force things away from him. All useful skills in battle. This one, however, was new to me.

I opened my mouth to push for more information but was interrupted by a deep growl. I quickly whipped around and again saw nothing.

"Alliard," I said, trying to swallow my fear. "Please tell me you heard that."

"Kind of hard to miss, Feyre."

Soon, one growl became two. Two turned into three. Three to four. Then it sounded like we were completely surrounded. Alliard slowly unsheathed his sword, keeping his other hand free so he could use his magic.

"Feyre, I need you to get out of here. Make a portal, go back to the inn. Something. Then send someone to help," Alliard ordered.

I formed two aether swords in my hands. "I'm not leaving you out here alone."

"My job is to keep you safe, so for once I need you to not argue with me and do as I say."

The idea of leaving him out here alone to run off and hide in the inn or get Father to get a team together terrified me. In that time he could die and I wasn't going to leave him here to die alone.

"You have no backup and there's no one around who's sober enough to fight. I'm training to fight. So I'm going to fight."

He opened his mouth to argue but was interrupted by the source of the sound stepping into the circle I'd created. They were the creatures we'd seen in the morgue in Artheas. Only these were alive and seemed to be out for blood. It swung its hand out, trying to slice me with its claws. I'd barely stepped back in time for it to miss me. There was no time for hesitation. If I hesitated, I'd get hit. So, I swung both my swords toward its neck.

I expected more resistance because of its armor-like skin, but my swords cut through it with ease. Its head rolled across the ground while its body folded in on itself and fell. Looking at the blood on my swords, I saw it wasn't red like it should have been. It was black.

There wasn't time for me to inspect it further as more of them had rushed into the circle. Alliard and I danced around, hacking and slashing at anything that got within a sword's length of us. We didn't stop moving.

Soon there was a small pile of bodies surrounding us, but that didn't stop them from coming. They simply stepped on the dead bodies, crushing them. Even over the hisses of pain and growls of frustration, I could hear the corpse's bones being broken. Whoever had control over these monsters made their mission clear. We weren't supposed to get out of this alive.

"Damn it!" I heard Alliard shout.

My swords sliced through another neck, cutting off another head as I looked over my shoulder. Alliard's sword had gotten stuck in a creature he'd downed and he couldn't get it to come loose. I watched as he focused a tunnel of wind in front of him, giving him time to pull one of his knives. I quickly downed two other creatures, giving me a small opening to rush over and assist him.

Together, we took down the three remaining creatures with ease. The other bodies were weighing down the body of the creature his sword was stuck in. Because of the added weight, he tugged the sword out with ease.

"Hold out your sword and keep them away from us," I ordered.

If we weren't in the situation we were in, I know he would've questioned me. He formed a bubble around us that had strong enough wind to slow down the incoming creatures. I carefully wrapped my hand around the tip of his sword and released a controlled stream of aether. The aether dripped down to the hilt, encasing it.

Ideally, I'd like to enchant it since I wasn't sure how long this would last. But, it would be better than nothing.

"Why?" Alliard asked.

"Because I've been cutting through them like butter and you're struggling. Aether to be helping in some way," I answered.

"Are you ready?" he asked.

"As ready as I'll ever be."

He dropped the bubble, exposing us to another handful of creatures. It took them a moment to realize nothing was hindering them anymore. By then, it was too late. Alliard and I killed them with ease.

We waited for more to rush us, but none came. Finally, they were all dead. I stopped counting the bodies when I hit thirty. My swords were covered in their thick, black blood. One look down at myself and I saw I was too. As my adrenaline lowered, I felt my skin burning beneath the sludge.

"Is it over?" I asked.

Alliard opened his mouth to respond but was silenced by the sudden appearance of portals. Three creatures who were significantly larger than the others stepped out. The ones dead at my feet were more human-sized, but these...these towered over Alliard at least by a foot. A smell wafted over the area that made me gag. It smelled like rotten meat.

"We'll need to work together on these guys," Alliard stated.

Two of the three monsters rushed Alliard and me while the third hung back. They were larger, but they were quicker. They both swung their arms towards us, forcing us to dodge the attack. Alliard and I were separated. There were a few feet between us now.

I hurriedly replaced one of my swords with a whip. This was a combination that Morana taught me. It was her go-to, and I remember her saying she thought I would like it too. I did, but I never got the opportunity to use it since it was difficult to do in the training room at home.

Now was as good a time as any.

I needed to use my size to my advantage. I lunged for the monster's legs. It seemed to pick up on my plan. It crouched down, allowing it to use its long arms to protect its legs. When I swiped at it with my sword, I grazed its arm. I jumped back, barely getting out of the way of its hit. I glanced over at Alliard, who was locked in a battle of his own.

He was moving quickly and landing many blows on the creature's legs. His speed made it hard for the creature to pinpoint him. With each cut, I could see the aether around his sword gradually growing dimmer. I wasn't sure how much longer it was going to last. I needed to finish off this monster and help Alliard before the aether could wear off entirely.

Working quickly, I struck with my whip, focusing my assault on the creature's torso. After a few hits, the creature curled in on itself protecting its torso, leaving its legs wide open. Without hesitation, I darted forward. I first cut its calm. It let out a loud scream enough to rattle all the surrounding building's windows. I was scared they'd shatter.

It stumbled forward, allowing me to pull my sword free and force it through its upper thigh. When I pulled my sword from its leg, arterial blood sprayed over my arm. I'd hit my target. My entire arm began burning, but I didn't have time to worry about that. I *needed* to get to Alliard.

The creature fell to the ground and as I turned, it used its remaining energy to wrap its hand around my calf, digging its claws into my skin. I went down with a scream as a searing pain shot up my leg. I ripped my let out of its grasp making its claws slide down my calf injuring me further.

"Feyre!" I heard Alliard shout.

"I'm fine!" I hastily called back. If he lost his focus, he could get hurt too.

My creature wasn't moving anymore and if it was, I couldn't tell. If it was still alive, I knew it would bleed out soon. My attention honed in on Alliard. He was slowing down. The creature could now keep up with him, and he could barely dodge its swings. I needed to help him.

Doing my best to ignore the searing pain in my ankle, I pushed myself up so I was standing. I couldn't put a lot of weight on my ankle, but just being up was better than nothing. I formed a small blade in my hand, lined it up with the creature's head, and threw it. The creature moved at the last minute, making my knife miss its mark and embed itself into its cheek. It grabbed its face with one hand, giving Alliard an opening.

He did his best to repeat what I'd done, but as his sword made contact with the creature, it swung its other hand down. With no other option, Alliard released his sword and jumped back. It wasn't enough, though. The creature's claws made contact with his shoulder, slicing him down to his hip.

"Alliard!" I shouted, my voice cracked.

My chest grew tight. I couldn't breathe. No matter how much I tried, I couldn't get air in. I could only manage shallow gasps. Panic engulfed me as I rushed over to his side. By the time I made it to him, the two living creatures disappeared through a portal.

Alliard was breathing, but barely.

"Alliard," I said, my voice trembling. "This might hurt a bit, but it'll hopefully buy us some time."

I laid my hands over his bloody torso and dug my fingertips into his wounds, letting my aether flow into him. Keeping in mind what Eos had told me, I didn't completely cauterize the wounds. I only did it enough to slow the bleeding. I hoped this would give me enough time to get him out of here.

Forming a portal on the nearest building, I made it lead to Artheas' hospital. The other victims were still there and where the research was taking place.

I got to my feet again, but this time I had to put weight on my injured ankle. I bit my tongue to keep from screaming, but it didn't stop the tears from flowing. I grabbed Alliard, trying my best to get him even partially through the portal. I got him to its opening before collapsing.

"Feyre? Is that you?" A voice called from behind me.

Looking over my shoulder, I could barely make out Dughall

with the help of my lingering aether orbs. There were a couple of people behind him, but I couldn't tell who they were.

"Dughall!" I shouted.

That was enough to get him to come running. He was kneeling by my side in the blink of an eye, leaving his friends wandering around to inspect the creatures' corpses. I guess the cat would be out of the bag on this one.

"I need...he needs..." I said through small sniffles.

"Shh, shh, shh. We'll get him through," he said, pulling me close. "Guys! Get him through the portal!"

The two rushed over instantly. One grabbed Alliard's arms, and the other grabbed his legs carrying him through its entrance. They reappeared a second later.

"Fey," Dughall said softly. "Fey, I need you to focus. What do you need us to do?"

I did my best to clear my head of my pain and panic so I could try to figure out what to do. The Council and Elders didn't want anyone knowing about the creatures, so I couldn't leave the bodies here. There wasn't long before sunrise therefore no time to get a team out here to remove all of the bodies.

"Burn the bodies. All except the large one over there," I said, pointing at it. "I need that one to go through the portal with us."

Dughall looked up at his friends. "You heard her. Go. And work quickly."

Again, they did as he said without hesitation.

"Can you walk?" Dughall asked me.

I shook my head.

Nervousness flashed through his eyes, but he did his best to mask it. "Alright. Okay. I'm going to pick you up and I'm sorry if I hurt you."

13.

Dughall was as gentle as he could be as he scooped me up. By the time he was standing upright, one of his companions was waiting with the larger creature to follow us through the portal. Dughall's eyes drifted down to my ankle.

"Oh god," he whispered.

It got him moving quicker. Two large strides was all it took to get us through the portal.

14.

"I don't want any signs that those bodies were there when you're done. And if you tell a soul about this, you'll be dead by sunrise." Dughall said to his friend.

He nodded. "Of course."

Dughall's companion turned on his heel and walked through the portal, closing it behind him. Soon I was swarmed by nurses who began poking and prodding at my ankle while asking enough questions to make my head spin. They talked over one another making it impossible to answer any. Csilla made an appearance and parted the sea of nurses. She let out a sigh of relief when she saw me alive and breathing.

"Thank you for giving us all a heart attack," she said. "We had a bloodied, wounded, and dying Alliard on our floor, a portal leading to god knows where, and no sign of you."

"I needed a bit of help, as you can see," I replied.

"Follow me. We've already got a room open and prepared for you," she sighed.

She led Dughall and me down a hallway, through a couple of large doors, into an empty room.

"Based on Alliard's wounds, I believe it's safe to assume that one of those creatures hurt your leg."

"It was. More specifically the one we dragged through the

portal. It isn't the same as the ones that attacked here."

"I'll get someone working on that and I'll have a doctor in here to clean your wounds."

She turned to leave, but before she could I asked, "How is Alliard."

Without looking at me, she said, "He's in surgery. I know you're aware that we have no way of dealing with the venom, so his chances of survival are low. The doctors will do everything they can to save him."

I didn't like hearing the truth. I wanted her to fill me with hope that he'd walk out of that operating room good as new. Csilla wasn't like that, though. She was always blunt as she didn't believe in sugar-coating things or beating around the bush.

Csilla left the room immediately after. Dughall carefully set me on the bed and pulled up a chair over to sit next to me. I wiggled, trying to get comfortable. I strained the crisp, white sheets with my blood as I fidgeted.

"You don't have to stay," I said.

"Let's go through tonight's events, shall we?" he replied. "Your guard is off in an operating room fighting for his life. You're here with your foot hanging on by a thread. And a couple of my friends are back in Khisfire, burning piles of unknown creatures that no one noticed invading town."

I raised an eyebrow. "And?"

"I'm not going anywhere until I know you're okay and I've been given some goddamn answers about all of this," he said firmly.

"You're going to be disappointed in that one. No one has answers right now."

"Then I'll be disappointed."

101

I smiled a little. "Thank you."

"We're friends and this is what friends do. We take care of each other."

A voice came from the doorway. "Oh thank god."

It was Eos. Behind her stood the doctor.

"Better behave yourself, Dughall. You're in the presence of an Elder now," I said.

"She's an Elder?" he said in disbelief. "She looks younger than I do!"

"Feyre, so far I'm approving of the company you keep," Eos said, laughing.

"Dughall this is Elder Eos. Eos, this is my wonderful friend Dughall."

"It's lovely to meet you," Eos said. "I thank you for helping Alliard and Feyre get here. Without you, well…I don't want to think about what could have happened."

"She would've done the same thing for me."

The doctor began looking at my ankle. His face dropped into a frown. That was enough to get my anxiety to spike.

"I want Eos to try using aether on me," I said, hastily.

"I cannot allow that." The doctor replied.

"I'm at a risk of dying anyway, so I might as well make it worth something," I argued.

"You're the only heir of Reidell. We are not risking your life."

"I'm not going to sit here and hope you can keep me alive long enough to find an antidote! We all know aether is special and unique so I am ordering you to let Elder Eos use her aether on me!"

"Princess—"

I narrowed my eyes. "Either let her do it or I'll do it myself as soon as you're gone."

14.

I watched as he weighed the options in his head. He slouched forward, shaking his head in defeat. "Fine. I'll allow her to try. But if I don't see results within the first minute, then it's done. I will have a guard come in here and handcuff you to the bed if I have to."

"Touch her and we're going to have issues, doc," Dughall said, eyeing him.

Eos stepped forward, giving me a quick wink as she sat on the edge of the bed.

"I'm going to take it slow. Tell me if you feel anything aside from the usual burn," Eos stated.

She put her hand on either side of my calf and let a small flow of aether out of her hands. I prepared myself for the burning sensation, but it didn't come. It felt warm and safe.

"There's no burn."

Eos nodded. "I'm going to use more aether."

I could see the increased flow of her magic and still no stinging or pain. I began feeling the burn a short while later. It was like a fiery brand touching my ankle. At first, it felt like the usual burn that came from aether but it quickly began to hurt like I stuck my leg in a fire.

"Burning!" I shouted.

She stopped. The doctor inspected my ankle. His eyebrows scrunched together. He laid his hand over my calf, closing his eyes for a second. They snapped open and he looked shocked.

"It worked," he said. I can't detect any poison in the wound anymore.

"Another win for Feyre," Dughall said, smirking.

"I need you to get me into the operating room with Alliard at once," Eos ordered.

"Give me a moment to heal her and I'll get you in there

immediately."

He carefully wrapped his hands around my calf and ankle. Within seconds, it looked like an ankle again, though it was scarred. I had expected it. My skin had been sliced to ribbons and healing could only do so much.

Eos took my hand in hers. "I'll do whatever it takes to get him out of that operating room alive."

Tears welling in my eyes, I said, "Thank you."

She and the doctor rushed out. I wasn't alone for long. Mother, Father, and Csilla entered the room soon after. My mother was the first to break free from the group. She rushed over to me and pulled me into a tight hug. I reciprocated. When she eventually let go, she took my hand in hers and wiped the tears off my cheeks.

"You must be Dughall," Father said.

"I am."

"Thank you for helping Feyre."

Father turned his attention to me. He opened his mouth to start interrogating me, but before he could I spilled my guts about almost everything. I tried speaking quickly, but I had to stop often to sniffle or because I lost my train of thought. I told them about how Dughall and I knew each other and the attack. However, I left out all mentions of Drystan. He didn't have anything to do with what was happening so there was no reason to bring his name into this.

"So, you've been feeding this man information?" Father asked sharply.

Mother spoke up before he could go on a rampage, "Zander, we can scold her about that later. There are more important things happening right now."

"We're talking about *treason*, Calla."

14.

"I understand that, but she was just attacked. That's a bit more of a pressing matter than treason."

Something flashed through Father's eyes. It was clear that he didn't want to talk about it, and I was inclined to agree. I'd love nothing more than to forget it entirely and instead focus on my betrayal. It was less terrifying.

"Did anyone know you were going to be in Khisfire?" Csilla asked.

"I didn't even know I was about until about five hours before I got there," I answered.

"When was the last time you visited?" Mother asked.

"She hasn't been in about four months," Dughall answered for me.

"What about these new creatures? What can you tell us about them?" Csilla asked.

"The scent of death followed them through the portal. There were three, though we were only able to take down one. The other two disappeared through the portal when they saw Alliard and I were no longer attacking. They were certainly smarter than the smaller ones."

"Smarter or not, they had to be following orders," Father said. "And if they *are* capable of taking orders without someone leering over their shoulder, it complicates things."

"Csilla, would it be possible to increase the number of guards in and around the hospital while Feyre and Alliard are here?" Mother asked.

She nodded. "I'll give the order as soon as we're done here. I already have people doing an autopsy on this new creature. Maybe we'll get something useful."

"When will Feyre be allowed to come home?" Father asked.

"Shouldn't be more than a few days," Csilla answered.

"Would you be willing to go wait for Alliard to get out of surgery?" I asked my parents.

"Are you sure you don't want one of us to stay here with you?" Mother asked.

I shook my head. "Dughall said he'd stick around for a bit. Alliard should wake up to familiar faces instead of being all alone."

Mother gave me a quick knowing look before nodding and pulling me into a tight hug. "Send someone to come get us if you need anything."

Father said nothing and didn't offer any affection of his own. Instead, he walked. Mother gave me a sad smile and followed him. Csilla offered a small smile and a nod before leaving, too. She wasn't big on physical contact, but that smile told me everything I needed to know—she was grateful to see I was okay.

"You and guard dog would make a cute couple," Dughall said once we were alone.

"We're just friends," I said, my face heating up.

Dughall rolled his eyes. "Oh please. Anyone with one eye and half a brain can see that you two are hot for each other."

"Please never use the phrase 'hot for each other' in my presence again."

He kept talking, ignoring me entirely, "They say near-death experiences really bring people together, so if he doesn't ask you out after this, he's even deeper in the sea of denial than you are."

"I liked it better when you were silent and moody."

"Feyre and guard dog sitting in a tree! K-I—"

"I will stab you if you keep going!" I shouted over him.

He let out a belly laugh. I thought he was going to fall out of his chair and start rolling around on the floor. I tried giving him the silent treatment, but his laughter was contagious. Soon we were both laughing so hard there were tears in our eyes.

Guilt seeped in, and I abruptly stopped. I shouldn't be laughing and joking right now. Even with Eos' help, there was no guarantee that Alliard would survive. If he died...it would be my fault. I'm the one who dragged him to Khisfire purely because I was tired of Father trying to protect me from what was going on. I should have taken him to Felluna or Dradour and actually given him a luxury vacation.

I should've done what every other spoiled, angry Princess would do and go spend an ungodly amount on clothes, shoes, and accessories. I could've bought Alliard whatever he wanted as payment for putting up with it. But I didn't do any of that. I took us to a small town in the middle of the woods so I could hang out with friends no one else knew about. Now he was fighting for his life and I was in here laughing and joking with another guy.

"Hey..." Dughall said.

The tears from the laughter quickly turned to those of fear, guilt, and sadness. Dughall quickly got to his feet, sitting on the bed next to me. He wrapped his arms around me tightly, trying his best to comfort me.

"It's okay Fey. Everything will be okay," he whispered.

I gripped his t-shirt tightly as I began sobbing into his chest, terrified of what tomorrow would bring.

15.

The next morning, I awoke in Dughall's arms. I still had his shirt clenched tightly between my fingers. Not wanting to wake him up, I slowly released the fabric and tried to slip unnoticed out of bed.

"Morning Princess," Dughall said, his eyes still closed.

"They didn't kick you out?" I asked.

He shrugged. "They tried, but you still had me in a death grip and I wasn't going to just walk out on you."

"Well, you're free to go now," I said, yawning.

"Thank god. I need a shower and food that doesn't smell like it's been sanitized," he said, standing up. "But more importantly, I need to start digging into this Drystan thing for you. So, if you don't hear from me for a few days, don't worry. I'm just in a work bubble."

"Let me know when you find something."

"I will. Send guard dog my best," he called over his shoulder as he left the room.

Once alone, I became painfully aware of how gross I felt. My face was tight from dried tears and snot. I was still caked in blood — it was anyone's guess whether it was mine, Alliard's, or the creatures'. I grabbed some clothes out of the bag my parents brought for me and disappeared into the bathroom to

15.

clean myself up. It took me scrubbing my skin raw to get all the black blood off my body, but I managed to do it.

Getting out of the shower, I inspected myself. Aside from the scarring on my calf and ankle, you would have never known I was in a battle last night.

When I emerged in fresh clothes and my hair twisted in a towel, I saw Eos and my mother sitting in my room. They were idly chatting and nothing about their demeanor gave away why they would be here. It made me nervous.

"What's going on?" I asked, slowly.

"Alliard's out of surgery. He's stable for now," Mother said.

"I cleansed him of as much poison as I could, but I wasn't able to get all of it. There was simply too much and we didn't want to push his body too far. Over the next few days, I'll slowly cleanse him and a doctor will heal his wounds," Eos explained.

I was sure that was the only reason Eos was here, but it couldn't be the whole reason Mother was. There was something guilt-like taking over her features.

"What's the bad news?" I asked.

Mother's eyes darted to the floor briefly before meeting mine.

"Well?"

"I don't want to argue with you considering everything that's just happened," she sighed, looking down again, unable to meet my eyes. "Your father and I discussed things. We've decided it would be best if you stay inside the palace. At least, until we have a better understanding of what's going on."

That was the last thing I wanted to hear right now. Someone clearly had it out for me and I didn't want to sit around the palace like a sitting duck. I wanted to be out there helping put a stop to this.

"What about my meetings with Eos?" I fumed.

"We've already discussed it and I have no problem coming to Reidell to meet you," Eos said.

"Will I be kept out of things that happen outside the War Room?" I asked.

"As much as your father would love to keep you far away from everything right now, you won't be. We know you need to be included to keep Eos up to date. You will be assigned multiple guards, though," Mother answered.

"Alright," I said. "I'll stay in the palace. For now."

Mother raised an eyebrow. "For now?"

"You can't keep me locked away and expect me to sit around after someone tried to kill me. Especially not after everything they've done," I hissed. "So, I'll do as you say for now. But don't think it will go on forever."

I expected her to be upset and begin lecturing me. Instead, she did the strangest thing. She started to laugh.

"I'm...I'm sorry," she hiccuped between laughs. "I'm supposed to be serious right now." She had to take a few deep breaths to collect herself, though giggles managed to slip out here and there. "It's just you sound exactly like I did when I was your age. So, because of that, I'll accept your answer and when you get tired of being on lockdown, we'll talk about it then. Sound good?

"I can live with that," I smirked. "Is there any word on how much longer I'm going to be stuck here?"

"You should be out in the next day or two. The doctor wants to monitor you to make sure there aren't going to be any side effects, so expect some nurses in and out. They said they are planning on taking blood samples and asking questions to monitor your recovery," Mother answered.

15.

Guilt flickered in her eyes as sadness turned down her lips. I recognized this look. It was the same expression Mother wore when she had to fulfill her Queenly duties and leave me behind.

"Go," I said.

"Are you sure?"

"There are more important things going on right now," I replied. "I'm alive and all healed up, so there's no need to sit around babysitting me."

She looked relieved as she pressed a quick kiss to my forehead. She said a quick goodbye to Eos, then rushed out of the room. Eos stayed behind. She eyed me like she knew one of my deepest, darkest secrets.

"What didn't you tell your parents?" she asked.

"I told them everything," I said, shrugging.

"I don't believe that," Eos stated. "Whatever it is, I won't tell anyone."

I paused and weighed my options. She was an Elder so she could prove to be useful. However, she could rat me out if she thought what I was hiding was too important to keep a secret. In the end, it was her wisdom and hope for her aid that outweighed my fear. I wanted answers.

"There's a rumor going around that Drystan is hiring mercenaries and criminals. No one knows why. Dughall is looking into it for me," I answered.

"Drystan isn't a saint; he's been in a fair amount of trouble. Perhaps he's using his new title of Prince to shelter him so he can continue his questionable activities."

"You know about his past?"

Like almost everyone in Moroluma, Drystan had a not-so illustrious past. He's been arrested a few times for petty crimes.

He's taken the blame for things he most likely didn't do so he wouldn't be seen as a snitch. When he became the heir to the throne and was forced to attend his classes at the academy, he cleaned up his act.

"The Elders and I did research on all of you once we decided to help you. We wanted to know who we were going to be working with," she answered. "I'd like it if you kept me in the loop with this, too."

"Am I allowed to ask why?"

"I don't trust Drystan because of his past, and if he's up to something involving criminals, I'd like to know."

"I will admit, I don't believe this is really him. He's enjoying the power and luxury that comes with being a Prince. He wouldn't mess that up now."

"I was under the impression that you'd be the last person to defend him."

"Don't get me wrong, I'm the last person who would ever consider him a friend. But I don't want to automatically assume the worst," I admitted. "But, if Dughall finds anything, I'll let you know."

~~~~~~~~~~~~~~~~

A couple of days had passed and I was finally getting released. As I pulled my shirt over my head, Dughall slipped into the room. I expected some sort of flirty comment, but, to my surprise, none came. Instead, I was treated to a stony, troubled expression.

"What's going on?" I asked.

"How much time do we have to talk?" he asked.

I shrugged. "I don't know. Mother is trying to get an update about Alliard before I get discharged. For both our sakes, I suggest you spit it out already."

15.

He looked like he was about to explode.

"Last night I was in the office late at night. I had some paperwork I had to do for new bonds that were filed today, boring stuff," He spoke so quickly that it was difficult to understand him. "A letter shot out of a portal, almost taking my eye out. It was from a friend of mine who runs a smaller mercenary organization. He knew I was looking into this Drystan shit because I'd asked him if he'd heard anything and he wasn't interested in what this letter was proposing, so he sent it my way. The letter had a date, time, and coordinates to meet at."

I waved my hands at him. "Whoa, whoa, whoa. Slow down. What letter? What makes you think it's connected to Drystan?"

"I asked around this morning and a lot of mercenary and criminal organizations got them. The letter was signed 'The Dark Prince.' Who else could that possibly be?"

"It could be anyone," I said, shaking my head. "When's the meeting?"

"It was an hour after my friend forwarded it to me. I gathered a couple of friends of mine, one of whom was there the night you were attacked, and we headed over."

"Did you see him?"

Dughall shook his head. "We spent all night searching those goddamned woods and there wasn't a sign of anyone or anything. We were either late or maybe by some awful miracle we were in the wrong spot."

I searched my brain. He had a letter telling him exactly where it was. It should have been impossible to mess that up. Then it hit me like a brick wall.

"Shadow magic!" I blurted.

"Alright now, I'm going to need you to explain that one to

me."

"One of Drystan's specialties is shadow magic. It allows him to hide himself and others in plain sight. That way no unwanted guests — such as yourself — can stumble upon his meeting. With that in mind, there were probably special instructions you missed that would allow you to get in," I said.

"How could I have possibly missed something when it was all laid out right in front of me?" Dughall snapped.

"Let me see the letter," I ordered, rolling my eyes.

He pulled it out of his pocket and slipped it into my hand. Touching it was enough to tell me what I needed to know. The realization made me chuckle.

"You idiot," I said, shaking my head while laughing. "You of all people should know what happened considering you use this trick every day."

He scrunched his eyebrows together in confusion. A second later, his eyes widened and he started laughing with me.

"Only the first person who opens the letter can see key information," he said. "I'm an idiot and should've realized that's what it was."

"If another letter pops up, get someone who can use shadow magic to take with you. With or without the special instructions, they should be able to spot the area for you and get you in."

"I'm sure I know an assassin or thief who uses shadow magic. I'll take a look through my contacts."

"Whoever you choose, just make sure you can trust them. The last thing we need is someone blabbing to anyone who'll listen."

"Feyre, oh Feyre. Everyone I know is a master at keeping secrets," he said. "If they weren't, we'd all be in prison."

15.

"I'm trusting you and your judgment with this. Don't make me regret it," I stated. "Also, any meetings from here on out will need to take place in the palace. I'm on lockdown again. I'll give your name and description to the guards so they'll know to let you in."

We grew quiet. It wasn't our usual comfortable silence. This one was awkward, filled with something I couldn't put my finger on, as we stood staring at one another.

"So...you're getting discharged today?"

I nodded. "No venom remains in my body, so aside from scarring, I'm good as new."

"And guard dog?"

"He's stable for now. They're still working on getting all the venom out of his body so they can heal him up, too. There's still plenty of time for something to go wrong."

I felt myself choking up again. Dughall took a few large strides across the room and pulled me tight against his chest.

"He's a fighter. He'll make it out of this alive," he whispered.

We stayed like that until I regained my composure. He slowly pulled away from me and took a few steps back.

Mother's voice cut through the room. "Ah, Dughall. I wasn't expecting to see you here again."

"Queen Calla," he said, bowing stiffly. It was off to see him acting respectfully. "I wanted to see how Feyre was and get an update on gua—Alliard."

"I assume Feyre had already filled you in," Mother said, coldly.

"She has."

"Then you'll have to excuse us. We need to get her discharged and hope ASAP."

Without protest, he gave me a small smile before leaving the

115

room. Mother stood in the doorway staring at me for what felt like lifetimes. I could feel her judgment. I could hear the rant before it even spilled past her lips.

"We're just friends so get that concerned...angry...Mother bear look off your face," I said. "And he's not a bad guy. Just because he's in a dangerous or questionable line of work doesn't mean he's some monster looking to use or hurt me."

Mother hastily raised her hands in surrender. "I trust your judgment, but you can't blame me for being protective and concerned given what's just happened."

I sighed heavily and grabbed my bag off the bed. I didn't want to think about that night anymore let alone talk about it.

"Let's get out of here, then. I'm tired of being in this hospital and the sanitary smell is making me nauseated."

16.

It had been four days since I'd been released from the hospital. Everything, for the most part, was fine. I would get occasional phantom pains if I stared at my scars for too long. Sometimes I couldn't help but stare at them. They were a reminder of the night I could have died.

I started wearing pants as often as I could so no one else could see them, either. If I wore a dress or skirt, then I wore tights, leggings, or boots that covered it. No one really seemed to know what was happening. If they did, no one brought it up. Aside from the guards, that is. They had been informed about what happened. Most looked at me differently now. As if they blamed me.

Alliard's survival was still uncertain. Mother had been in constant contact with Csilla, who gave updates. Today was supposed to be the day Alliard would be cleaned and healed completely. It didn't mean he'd be out of the woods, yet. The doctors were still concerned that Eos wouldn't be able to cleanse him entirely of the venom and that there would be side effects. All we could do was wait and see.

I walked into my parents' office where they were both staring intensely at a paper on the desk.

"What ya got there?" I asked, taking a seat.

"It's an inventory list that Demir sent over," Mother answered.

"What wonderful creations are we getting this time?"

"Armor and weapons," Father said. Father looked up, his eyes boring into mine. "Your mother told you about how you're confined to the palace, yes?"

"She has," I nodded. "I hope she passed on my response."

"She did. When you get tired of being in the palace, we'll sit down and see where things are at," he said. "Now. We have something important to discuss."

My heart dropped to my stomach.

"Yes?"

"Why did you add Dughall to the list of people approved to enter the palace?" he asked, calmly.

I wanted to throw up. I'd hoped that he wouldn't check that list.

"You've been feeding this man information for who knows how long regarding god knows what, and now you're expecting us to allow him to waltz into the palace?" he asked sharply. Father's calm exterior was cracking.

"He's given me just as much information in return, if not more. Thanks to him, I know what's going on in all the corners of Etrayus since you're picky about when I get to know things."

"That's your excuse for treason?" Father scoffed. "You wanted information about Etrayus?"

"You pick and choose what information I'm told because you want to protect me and shield me from the horrors of the world! You expect me to be prepared to rule a Kingdom, but you won't stop treating me like I'm a child!"

"We're your parents, Feyre. It's our job to protect you," Mother said, cutting in.

16.

"I understand you're doing what you think is best for me and I understand you're trying to protect me, but I'm not a normal child. I'm a future Queen. How do you expect me to handle running a Kingdom and a country when you aren't open and honest with me about everything?" I asked, exasperated.

"Honesty is a two-way street, Feyre," Father stated. "You should have come to us instead of going to a stranger or at least came clean about what you were doing sooner."

"Why are you putting him on the list anyway? What's so important that he needs to be able to stop by whenever he sees fit?" Mother asked.

I was already in trouble and they were already upset with me. Things couldn't get much worse from here.

I let out a small sigh and told them everything. I felt like they would brush it off and let me have my suspicions. It wasn't like I was going to blindside Drystan and accuse him to his face. My suspicions were going to stay with me.

Mother let out a breathy laugh. "You can't possibly think he'd be involved in something so terrible. Morana keeps that boy on such a tight leash that he would have no way to slip back into his old ways."

I shrugged. "You two kept me on a tight leash and I still got myself into trouble."

"She's for a point there," Father said. "I still remember when she found a way around the portal locks that one night. We could never figure out how she did that."

"But why have Dughall look into it?" Mother asked. "Unless you think there's something more sinister going on."

I shook my head quickly. "Of course not. But if he's diving back into the criminal world or someone's impersonating him, I'd like to know for peace of mind."

"Alright," Mother said before Father could speak. "If this is something you feel you need to do then we won't stop you."

Father nodded. "Let us know if he comes back with anything."

"Um. Yeah. Sure," I said, feeling shocked. I assumed they'd brush me off and ignore the whole thing. "I'm going to go rest until dinner if that's alright."

Mother pulled me into a tight hug. When we began to pull away, another set of arms wrapped around us. My father's musky cologne filled my nose, making me smile. For a moment, it felt like everything was okay and this was a normal afternoon.

"It's good to have you back in one piece," Father whispered.

We stayed in our group hug for a bit longer. I flashed them a large smile when we detangled from each other and made my way to my bedroom.

~~~~~~~~~~~~~~~~

There was a loud pounding on my door that jolted me out of my sleep. The sun was just now starting to set. There was no way I'd overslept. I tried wrapping my brain around why someone could possibly be waking me up. The pounding continued while I tried wracking my brain, making me bristle with irritation.

"Alright! Alright!" I shouted. "I'm coming!"

I pulled myself out of bed, mumbling a string of curses. I swung the door open and was greeted by a guard. My heart stuttered as my brain conjured up every negative thing that could be happening.

"King Zander wishes to see you in the War Room immediately," he stated.

"Do you know why?" I asked frantically.

He shook his head. "I was only ordered to come bring you

down to the War Room at once."

"Okay. Thank you."

He bowed then stepped to the side so I could walk out of my room. I ran to the basement afraid of what news awaited me. The guard kept right in step with me but didn't say a word.

It was impossible to remain positive. Anxiety filled my head with terrifying narratives. By the time I slipped through the War Room's door, I was practically hyperventilating. Searching the room, I noticed Demir was nowhere to be found.

"What's going on?" I asked frantically.

"There was another attack," Father said.

Morana shook her head. "Those creatures attacked the caravans Demir sent — with the weapons and armor. Everyone was killed."

"In broad daylight!" Csilla exclaimed. "We've assumed these things were nocturnal since the other attacks only occurred after sunset. We should've known better."

More attacks. More innocent lives were lost. More families torn apart. It seemed things were getting worse and there was no sign of them getting better.

"I also have some news, though I'm afraid it isn't anything good," Amara said. "I've been analyzing the plants from the academy and Artheas. They've been poisoned by whatever coats the creature's claws. It seems that if it is alive, then it can be poisoned and killed."

"More questions and no answers," Father sighed.

"Do the Elders have anything?" Drystan asked.

His question drew everyone's gaze, but only for a brief second. Attention quickly turned to me since I was their connection to the Elders.

"Eos said she'd contact me when they have something," I said.

"So what are we supposed to do in the meantime? Sit around watching everyone around us get attacked and killed? Wait until they come after the rest of us?" Drystan asked. The anger in his voice made me tense up.

"Those are excellent points, Drystan. And my response would be that we need to put all of Etrayus on lockdown until further notice," Father said.

Morana scoffed, "You can't be serious, Zander."

"I'm incredibly serious. Drystan is right. We're all at risk now. If we go on lockdown, we can increase guard presences everywhere which would allow us to keep a closer eye on everything," Father said. "I'd also like to come clean to everyone about the other attacks and everything else we've been hiding."

The room erupted with protests.

"We've kept it hidden for a reason!" Morana shouted.

"And maybe we shouldn't have!" Amara shouted back.

"To protect everyone, they need to know what we're up against!" Father exclaimed.

Csilla tried throwing her two cents into the mix, but everyone else spoke over her. She sat back and observed with Drystan and I.

Morana rose from her chair. "Telling everyone would simply cause panic!"

Father rose from his chair too. "We wouldn't have to worry about that with lockdowns and curfews and restrictions!"

Amara tried shouting over both of them but was drowned out too. Soon Father and Morana's voices melded together as they matched each other's temper and volume. It was impossible to make out what they were saying. All we could do was sit back silently hoping it wouldn't get physical.

"Morana! Enough!" Father growled. "I have made my

decision and you will fall in line and accept it!"

They were both panting now. Morana had a darkness swirling in her eyes. She was clearly far from done with this argument, but she paused, visibly weighing her options. Father, as the ruler of the capital of Etrayus, had more pull than the others. Usually, he didn't use it as he preferred for everyone to be on board with something to avoid what was currently happening.

A heartbeat passed and Morana sat down, doing her best to hide all emotion in her face. And failing. Her jaw was still too tight and her body was noticeably tense.

"Would anyone else like to argue about this, or can we begin planning this meeting?" Father asked. He was still standing, staring down everyone at the table. His eyes darted around daring anyone to push further. No one did. "Good," he said as he took his seat. "Let's begin."

They began working out the details as if nothing happened while Drystan and I listened.

17.

Tensions were high all across Etrayus. In only two days, all Kingdom, town, and city officials had pulled together to prepare for the lockdown which would start tonight. Strict rules had been created and would be posted on every street corner, and everyone's common space.

Morana had brought several specialists in illusion magic who would allow us to project our meeting all across Etrayus, ensuring everyone would be able to watch the meeting unfold. It was going to be a stressful day.

The Council, joined by Drystan and I sat in the conference room in the back of the Courthouse. We waited anxiously for the clock to strike nine o'clock. I kept getting flashbacks to the meeting we had a few weeks after the academy attack. That one didn't end well and I was sure that this one would end the same, if not worse.

"Remember, we need to get the information out as quickly and concisely as possible. If we get interrupted by the crowd, we redirect their attention to the reason we're all here and continue on," Father instructed.

"And if that doesn't work?" Demir asked.

He was still on edge from the attack of his caravans. His blacksmiths and enchanters were crafting weapons and armor as quickly as possible, aware that we needed it now more than ever. We'd have guards on patrol in every nook and cranny, so we needed them to be as safe and protected as possible.

"The guards have strict instructions to do whatever it takes to get people under control, Even if they have to drag people out," Father answered. His eyes darted up to the clock. "Feyre. Drystan. Go ahead and get out into the courtroom, the meeting starts in a few minutes."

Drystan had agreed to sit in the back of the courtroom next to me. We were sandwiched together between two guards, both guards had the same instructions Alliard did at the last meeting; if anything goes wrong, they get us out of there immediately.

We slipped through the courtroom keeping our heads down. It looked like it was more packed than it had been last time. I didn't know it was possible, but it clearly was. Drystan and I made it to our seats and settled in. Council filed from the back and took their seats.

My mind then drifted to Alliard. He was the only one who was missing today. It felt wrong to be doing this without him. He should be here. He should be my guard today.

I blinked away the tears forming in my eyes focusing on Father who wasted no time addressing the crowd.

"You have all been waiting for updates, answers, and justice. Unfortunately, we won't be able to give you all of that today. In fact, some of you most likely will leave here more upset than when you arrived. Keeping that in mind, we request that you stay calm and quiet so we can tell you everything we need to tell you."

Csilla took over from there. "A couple of weeks ago after the sun had set, Artheas was attacked. Waves of masked, unknown people and horrifying monsters came through portals. They attacked anyone and everything they could find. They destroyed houses, restaurants, and even went after the temple. Many lives were lost, but few from the enemy side. Some were merely injured, but that created another problem. The creatures have venom coating their claws and in their saliva. Anyone bitten or scratched was infected and we were unable to cleanse them or heal their wounds. We were left scrambling to figure out how to heal them while also keeping them from succumbing to their wounds."

I watched people in the crowd exchanging glances, but no one tried to interrupt.

Amara stood next. "Thanks to Elder Eos, we learned that aether and angelic light can be used to cleanse the venom. It is a slow process, but it works, which is all that matters," Amara said, smiling. "Now, we all know how rare aether and angelic light users can be, so Elder Eos is assisting Felluna to create an antidote based on those skills. It's going slow, but things are looking hopeful."

Waves of chatter could be heard throughout the room. I sat up a little straighter already expecting the worst. Then Morana rose from her seat which was enough to quiet things down.

"Alongside Moroluma, Queen Amara learned that this venom doesn't just affect humans. It also affects the earth itself. It can kill grass, flowers, bushes, trees, et cetera. The venom moves too quickly for us to stop it. This could be extremely dangerous for something like The Enchanted Forest. We're still trying to find a way around this, but as of now we have nothing to share."

Father reclaimed the stage as he began talking about the night Alliard and I were attacked. I knew he'd be speaking about it. I had spent all night mentally preparing myself for it.

17.

I thought I'd prepared well, but as he spoke my heart started beating a little faster and my calf began throbbing. My palms grew slick with sweat. I tried wiping them on the skirt of my dress, but they remained damp.

Then Father said Alliard's name and began talking about his injuries. Any composure I might have had slipped as images of Alliard's injured, bloody body flashed through my head. Looking down at my hands, I could see blood coating them and dripping onto the wooden floor beneath me. I imagined Alliard fighting for his life on the operating table as doctors tried to save him.

I balled my hands into fists and dug my fingernails into my palms trying to take deep breaths to calm myself. I was doing my best to resist the urge to bolt out of the courtroom entirely. I felt someone's elbow dig into my rib cage jarring me back into reality. Drystan glanced my way.

"Are you back with us?" he whispered.

I slid closer to my guard as my mind registered that he was touching me.

Without looking at him, I said, "Yes."

He gave me a small nod and turned his attention back to the meeting. I was able to refocus and listen to Demir talk about the attack on the caravans.

"It's clear that this is only going to continue to escalate until we find the people behind this," Father said. "With this in mind, we have decided to put Etrayus on lockdown."

"We will be increasing the number of guards everywhere. They will keep detailed logs and if anything occurs, we will let you all know," Demir stated.

"The rules of this lockdown will be posted. Copies will also be sent to everyone," Morana said. "We are asking that no one goes anywhere alone, nor leave their houses until the set hours of freedom. We also ask that you report anything you consider odd to a guard. There is to be absolutely no traveling. If we catch you breaking the rules we will give you a warning the first time, but any time after that, you risk being arrested."

"We apologize for hiding these things from you and we hope you're able to forgive us," Amara said. "Thank you all for letting us explain everything and thank you in advance for complying with the rules of the lockdown. This concludes our meeting."

I expected people to be outraged, but no one spoke. The courtroom was so silent you could hear a feather drop. Council rose from their seats and returned to the back of the courthouse. Drystan, our guards, and I all rose in unison fleeing the courthouse hastily so we wouldn't get stuck in the crowd. Drystan and I separated and slipped into our own coaches.

I expected the same silence I experienced on the way to the courthouse. To my surprise, he decided to strike up a conversation.

"Has Alliard really been fighting for his life? Or was that just for shock value to get everyone to adhere to the lockdown?" he asked.

I didn't want to have this conversation. Not now. Not ever again.

"No one gave you all the gory details?" I asked quietly.

He shook his head. "We were only told that you two had been attacked and hospitalized. But you're fine, so we weren't sure what the truth was."

I looked down at my shoes as I spoke. "It sliced him open from shoulder to hip. They were able to stabilize him and Elder Eos began cleansing him of the venom. He's supposed to get his last round of cleansing today or tomorrow, but even then they aren't sure if he's out of the woods yet."

"So you did stand there and do noth—" He cut himself off when he heard the anger in his voice. "I apologize, Princess. I shouldn't speak to you that way."

That's when I realized why every guard in the palace had been giving me weird looks. They all believed that the helpless Princess stood by letting their friend and colleague get attacked.

"I was fighting another monster when I realized he was in trouble," I said, my voice cracking. "I downed it as quickly as I could and tried to get to him to help, but the creature grabbed my leg, tearing it open. That was enough of a distraction to put Alliard in harm's way. It's my fault." My tears were flowing freely now and I didn't bother trying to stop them. "So anything you and your friends have said about me or thought about me, I've probably said it to myself already. I know it's my fault and I will spend every day wishing I could change what happened."

We went quiet. He didn't ask me any more questions, and I didn't offer more information. When we arrived at the palace, he walked me down to the basement. I took a moment to collect myself outside of the War Room. Once I had mostly dried my tears, I stepped inside where everyone had gathered.

"That went better than I expected," I said as I sat.

"Yeah. I wasn't expecting them to be so silent at the end," Drystan said.

"It was a lot of information to process and take in," Amara replied. "I'm just glad they allowed us to speak uninterrupted."

"Alright," Father said, interrupting the conversation. "Does anyone have questions before it's time to begin the lockdown?"

Morana raised a few fingers. "Are you sure you only want

our updates and logs once a week?"

Father nodded. "For now, that seems like it will be enough. If there's an increase in odd activities or attacks, we'll increase it."

"How long will it take to get all the guards equipped with the new armor and weapons?" Csilla asked.

"Everyone should have what they need by the end of the week," Demir answered. "If anyone finds themselves missing anything, contact me and we'll get it to you immediately."

There were no further questions.

"Go back to your homes then. It's time for the lockdown to begin," Father ordered.

18.

Reidell hasn't been this quiet since everything began. I didn't wake up to protesters screaming outside the palace gates. There were no guards shouting. I couldn't see people scurrying past the crowds.

It had been even longer since I'd seen Etrayus as it usually was. Children excitedly peering through the palace gates. People selling their wares on the sidewalk, people rushing to get to work on time. The happiness that flourished in Reidell was gone. It had been replaced with fear and frustration.

It was heartbreaking to see.

With nothing to watch from the windows, I found myself aimlessly wandering through the palace. Occasionally, I stopped to make small talk with the guards and staff members. Some of them were nice enough to stop and talk to me for a bit, but some wouldn't even look at me. They were still upset over Alliard. I didn't blame them. I carried on and tried to not dwell on it.

It wasn't long before I found myself in the library. I used to spend all my time there when I was younger with Merindah and Mother. When they were teaching me how to be a proper lady, we did my lessons here. I spent most of the time running around, jumping on the couches, and climbing the ladders for the bookcases instead. I would climb to the top and no one could convince me to climb down until Father swooped in and saved the day.

As I got older and my training moved to the academy, I stopped spending time here. I spent so much time cooped up in the library at the academy that when I came home, the last thing I wanted was to spend more time in a library. Looking at it now, though, it made me sad that I stopped visiting. It was a beautiful, peaceful place.

It has two stories. The first was more open, leaving room for a sitting area in the center with couches. Some tables and chairs were placed at the side of the room. Large bookcases overtook the other walls, broken up on the far wall by large floor-to-ceiling windows. The natural light made it bright and airy. The second floor, however, was my favorite. It had the same large windows, but the bookcases created a lot of nooks and crannies to hide away in. Each one had a large chair, couch, or piles of pillows and blankets to curl up in.

That's where I found myself. I flopped into a large, plush chair that was almost more comfortable than my own bed. I had a fuzzy blanket wrapped around me and I was ready to doze off for the afternoon. Someone called my name from downstairs as I was at the brink of being pulled into dreamland.

"Feyre! Feyre, are you in here!"

"Up here!" I shouted back, dragging myself out of the chair.

I leaned over the railing to see Merindah standing in the center of the downstairs area. It was a pleasant surprise.

"Your parents need you in the entryway. It seems Elder Eos is looking for you," she said.

"And here I was thinking you simply missed me and wanted to make sure I was okay," I replied.

18.

She smiled. "I have and I would, but I almost have a job to do, which at this moment is to get you to the entryway."

"I'll hold you to that at a later date then," I said, returning her smile.

I bee-lined for the stairs and jogged all the way out to the entryway. If Eos was here that had to mean that she had more information. I didn't want to waste any time.

When I made it to the edge of the grand staircase, I almost stopped in my tracks. Standing with my parents and Eos was Alliard. He looked fragile. There were dark circles under his eyes. His cheeks were hollow and he, in general, looked frail.

Feeling a bit awkward and unsure of myself, I approached slowly hoping to not draw Alliard's attention to me.

"Ah, Feyre," Eos said, smiling. "I hope I didn't interrupt anything."

I shook my head. "Not at all. I was just spending some time in the library."

My eyes darted over to Alliard. He was already staring at me. Our eyes locked long enough to be aware of the other staring. We quickly looked away from each other. Now wasn't the time for the conversation we needed to have.

"I hope that means you're willing to take some time to speak with me. We have a few things to discuss," she said.

"I'm more than willing," I said, probably a bit too quickly. "Anything is better than making another loop around the palace," I added with a small laugh.

"Then lead the way."

I glanced at Alliard one last time. He was talking with my parents now, so he didn't notice. I stuffed my feelings of guilt away into a tightly sealed box and wrapped it in chains as I led Eos to the library. Once inside, we sat on separate couches with only a coffee table between us.

"I figured we could start with what you'd really like to know about," she said. "He's completely cleansed of the venom from what we can detect and we have seen no signs of side effects. He will need a bit of extra rest because we pushed his body farther on the last day of healing than we should have. But that's about it. He'll be good as new before you know it."

That had to be what my parents were discussing with him. Hearing that, they'd want to keep him off duty as long as they could.

"Thank you for taking care of him. I have no idea what I'd do if he didn't make it…" I railed off, my last words a little more than a whisper.

Eos smiled softly. "You really care for this boy, don't you?"

"He's been a good friend to me."

There was a glint in her eyes telling me she had more to say, but she let it go.

"I have a few questions to ask before we really get down to business, if you don't mind," she said.

I nodded. "That's fine."

"They're about the night you were attacked. If you need a minute between questions or before you answer, just say so. I understand that night was extremely traumatic for you and the last thing I want to do is make it worse."

I nodded. While I hated thinking or speaking about it, I knew that even the smallest detail could be useful.

"You said the three larger creatures seemed to be more intelligent. How did you reach that conclusion, exactly?"

"They had a…pack mentality? That's the only real way I can think to describe it. They came in as a group. One hung back while the other two attacked. As soon as Alliard and I were no longer a threat to them, they retreated. They didn't stick around to see if we lived or died. They got out of there quickly."

"Would you say they seemed to be following orders?"

I nodded. "Both sets of creatures seemed to be. The smaller ones seemed like mindless drones, though."

"This is the last question, and I know you've already answered this but I only want to make sure you haven't remembered anything new," Eos said. "Did anyone or *could* anyone have known you were going to be in Khisfire that night?"

"There's no way," I said firmly. "Like I said, I didn't even know I was going to be there just before we left. No one could have known. All I said was that I was going away for the weekend."

"You didn't give any specifics?"

"Not until Alliard and I were in the coach together and I told the driver where to take us. But there was no one around, so no one could have heard."

She nodded. "Alright. I'll leave it there for now and tell you what I've found out."

I relaxed, but not enough. I still felt on edge because I knew whatever she told me couldn't be anything good.

"We did an autopsy and ran some tests on that larger creature you brought in. Between the autopsy and the DNA, everything came back with one obvious answer. That *thing* was once human."

"What about the smaller ones?" I asked.

"We re-ran our initial tests and compared everything to the larger ones," she sighed. "It's not conclusive. They have similarities but not enough to one-hundred percent, without a doubt confirm our hypothesis. We can say that they must have been created, though. They were certainly not summoned."

"Do we have any idea how they were created?"

"That's what we're trying to figure out. The type of magic and rituals needed to do something like this…they aren't humane."

We grew silent as I took in the information. The library doors opened and the sound of heavy, hurried footsteps stole my attention. I didn't have to wonder for long to see who it was. Barely a heartbeat passed before Dughall was standing in front of us.

"What are you doing here?" I asked.

"I have information you might need now rather than later," he said hastily.

I could feel the anxiety tolling off him in waves.

"Sit. Talk," I ordered.

"Dughall, right?" Eos said.

He nodded. "Right. It's nice to see you again."

Eos motioned for him to keep talking. "Well, go on. Don't leave us in suspense."

"The Dark Prince, whoever he may be, is having another meeting tomorrow night," he said. "This time I received my own letter."

"Are you sure it's the same person?" I asked.

"Same handwriting. Same signature. I had a handwriting expert I know look at them. He confirmed it."

"Do you know how many letters were sent out?" I asked.

"No clue. But I asked around to see if anyone I knew got one. Some of them got one for the last meeting, chose to ignore it, and got another one."

"Whoever this is, is stubborn, I'll give them that."

"You're still hiding something, Mr. Dughall," Eos stated.

"Dughall?" I said.

"I don't have much information, so I can't confirm anything.

18.

But some of the people who are part of organizations that attended the last meeting are missing. I've tried asking around, but no one is confirming or denying anything. The few — the very few — people who were willing to say anything to me, though, said they haven't heard from them."

Fear struck me in my core, sending a shiver down my spine.

"We need names, descriptions, and DNA or fingerprints or something along those lines if possible," I stated.

"Feyre, you don't think..." Eos trailed off.

"I do think. This can't be a coincidence," I said firmly. "If you're going to take people and do who knows what experiments on them, who do you use? Mercenaries. Assassins. Thieves. Low-life criminals. People that no one can confirm or deny if they're really missing or not. People that no one will care about if they do go missing."

"I can get people working on that today, but what do you want me to do about the meeting tomorrow night?"

"Get names of everyone there or at the very least extremely detailed descriptions. And get us something that we can use to identify whoever is holding these meetings," Eos ordered.

"And don't start a fight with anybody. Act like you're genuinely interested in joining their little cult and play nice for once," I said.

He nodded. "The meeting is at midnight. I'll come straight here when it's over."

Eos grimaced. "You can contact me at a decent hour."

I suppressed a laugh and nodded. "Of course."

"Also, keep this part of the conversation from your parents. But do tell them about the creatures. Maybe Amara can figure something out. Or maybe Morana knows something about summoning creatures that we don't," Eos said. "With that, I should get back to Felluna. We're still working on the antidote."

"Thank you for stopping by." I smiled. "I'll talk to you in a couple of days."

"Stay safe, Feyre."

With that, she formed a portal, stepped through, and disappeared. Once along with Dughall, I quickly filled him in and shared our concerns. If he was going to be helping us by going to that meeting, I wanted him to know exactly what was going on. The last thing I wanted was for him to get hurt, killed, or —God forbid — used in whatever experiments they were doing.

"If you want to back out now or tomorrow, I'll understand," I said at the end.

"I'm not stopping until this whole nightmare is over," Dughall said firmly.

"Then be careful," I said. "If there are any signs of things getting out of hand, just get out of there. We can always find another way to see if Drystan is behind those meetings, but there's no finding another you."

Dughall smirked. "Keep this up, Feyre, and I'll start thinking you're falling in love with me."

While I appreciated his attempt to lighten the mood, it didn't lessen my nerves any. Instead of giving him a classic witting or sarcastic response, I reached over and pulled him into a tight hug.

"I've already almost lost one friend; I can't go through that again with you," I whispered.

He wrapped his arms around me just as tightly. "Nothing is going to happen to me. I'll come back in one piece, I promise."

19.

After Dughall and I had our moment, he left to get to work. I stayed in the library only I went back up to the second floor to curl up in my large chair. Unfortunately, dinner came around quicker than I wanted, forcing me out of my hiding place. I filled my parents in on the information I could tell them over our meal. I didn't say much else. As soon as I finished eating, I excused myself to hide away in my room for the rest of the night.

Tomorrow night could change a lot and I wasn't sure how to feel about it. I didn't want to think Drystan could be behind any of this or could know some. I didn't like him by any means, but that didn't mean I believed he was capable of any of this. All I could do was hope that whatever Dughall was able to dig up could exonerate him.

Taking a deep breath I let my eyes drift closed. No more thinking for me tonight. I knew that I'd spend tomorrow an emotional, anxious wreck, so tonight I'd do my best to relax. After a few minutes, I realized that laying here wasn't going to do anything for me, so I decided to take a bath. I went to my bathroom and started pulling out some of my candles, bath salts, and my jars of dried flower petals. There was a knock at my door as I pulled the last of my jars out.

I bit my tongue resisting the urge to scream at them to go away. Taking another deep, stabilizing breath, I dragged myself to the door. My heart dropped to the pit of my stomach when I saw Alliard standing on the other side. He looked better rested than before but still looked frail.

"You look shocked to see me," he said.

"I assumed my parents would've put you on a lockdown of your own until they deemed you fit for duty," I replied.

"They only said I had to stay on palace grounds. They also asked me to not jump straight into my usual workout routine, so I wouldn't strain myself."

I stepped to the side. "Now that I know you won't get me in trouble by being here, you can come in."

Alliard laughed as he walked in. "Me? Get you in trouble?"

I shut the door behind him while he got himself comfortable at the edge of my bed. He braced his back on one of the bedposts. I sat across from him, wringing my hands together and trying to not look at him. This conversation was destined to get serious, and I was dreading it.

"Feyre," Alliard said gently. "You know we have to talk about this."

I focused on my duvet. "Then talk."

"What happened after I went down?" he asked.

"You don't know?"

He shook his head. "I tried getting Elder Eos or Queen Calla to tell me, but I was in and out of it most of the time I was in the hospital. If they told me, I don't remember it."

"The two remaining creatures retreated into a portal. I rushed over to you, used my aether to cauterize your wounds to try to slow the bleeding, and then formed a portal to Artheas' hospital. I couldn't get you through on my own. Dughall and some of his friends were able to help us both. By the time I got through, you were in surgery and I was whisked off to a room of my own."

"They said that if you hadn't used your aether I wouldn't have lived long enough to get to the operating table."

"It's my fault you had to be on the operating table in the first place," I mumbled.

"Feyre. Don't go there," Alliard said firmly.

"Don't go where?"

"This wasn't your fault."

My eyes snapped up to meet his as the frustration and guilt rose to the surface. "How is it not!" I shouted. "I'm the one who dragged you to Khisfire! I'm the one who dragged you out to a bar! I'm the one who kept us out so late that there wasn't anyone around to help when things went wrong! And those things were after me! Me! Not you! All you did was get in their way and you almost died because of it!"

"And you had no idea it was going to happen!" he shouted back. "You didn't know they'd be after you! You didn't know they would attack you! And you didn't know they'd be so hellbent on killing me too instead of just focusing on you!"

"You...you almost died," My voice cracked.

Before I could stop them, tears spilled out of my eyes. The emotions surrounding our attack that I'd been trying to hide all came flowing out. I was feeling everything at once. All the anger. All the sadness. All the anxiety and frustration. All the confusion. All the pain.

I felt the bed shift and then I felt Alliard's arms wrap around me. He pulled me into his chest and gently rubbed my back, doing his best to comfort me.

"I'm right here Feyre. I'm in one piece. I'm not hurt anymore.

I'm alive," he whispered.

That only made me cry harder. He wrapped his arms around me tighter. He let me get out all of my emotions as he whispered sweet words of affirmation into my ear. I wasn't sure how long he held me, but slowly the tears stopped and I pulled myself together.

I took a few deep breaths as my hands found his chest. Alliard released me as he stood. I watched as he disappeared into the bathroom, only to return with a wet rag in his hands. He sat down beside me and gently grasped my jaw to hold my face steady. He wiped the tears and snot from my face. I was too drained to insist that I was capable of it myself. So, I sat there silently letting him do it for me.

"I don't want you blaming yourself for this anymore," Alliard said firmly.

"Alliard—"

"No," he said. "Unless you're hiding something from me, there's no way you could have known that any of this was going to happen. There's nothing you could've done to prevent it or stop it. I let myself get distracted and I let myself get hurt."

I pulled my bottom lip between my teeth and let out a small sigh of defeat. "Fine."

"Good."

He still had my face in his grasp as we stared at each other. I watched his eyes flick down to my lips, lingering there for a few heartbeats. His gaze darted back up to meet mine. My chest rose and fell a little quicker with anticipation.

Instead of leaning forward like I hoped, he dropped his hand and cleared his throat.

"Um," he said, clearing his throat again. "Catch me up on what's been happening. All of Etrayus is on lockdown. So,

19.

clearly, I missed something big.

Awkwardness hung in the air between us, but I did my best to ignore it as I filled him in. I told him about tomorrow night's meeting and Dughall's plan to come by afterward. I followed that but up with his sword secrecy since Mother and Father didn't know.

"I'd like to be there when Dughall comes by, if that's alright," Alliard said.

"Of course," I said, a bit too eagerly. "We're meeting in the library. I'm sure I'll be in there way before the meeting even starts out of anxiety."

"I'll join you when I can. I asked some of the guys to train with me in their off time so I can whip myself back into shape. It will be before dinner, so it'll depend on how long we go for."

I nodded. "Sounds like a plan.

Uncomfortable silence spread between us as he met my eyes again. There was something in his expression that told me he wanted to say something more. Every fiber of my being was begging him to. He didn't seem to get my telepathic message since he stood up.

"Well. Uh. I should probably get back to the barracks," he said. "Ya know. Eat some food. Continue resting."

"Yeah," I said, sounding distant. I cleared my throat. "Yeah. Of course."

Alliard leaned down, pressing a gentle kiss to my forehead. When he pulled away, I opened my mouth to say something. He was gone before I found the courage to speak. My eyes lingered on the door. Rejection washed over me as my stomach twisted into a knot. Slowly, I got to my feet.

I dropped the wet rag into my hamper, then resumed filling up my bathtub. I sprinkled in a cup of bath salts and various flower petals. I silently prayed they'd do what they were supposed to and lift my mood or help me relax. God knows I needed it now more than ever.

20.

There were twelve hours until the meeting started. But it was who knows how many hours until Dughall would actually arrive. He'd sent a letter this morning reiterating that he'd be by afterward, so I better find a way to stay awake and wait for him. He also mentioned that his men had been able to find some information that Eos and I asked for. I wanted to contact Eos as soon as I'd read it, but I stopped myself. There was no point in contacting her until I had the information in my hands.

Excitement and anxiety blended together ensuring I wouldn't be able to sit still. I wandered through the palace, hoping that if I walked enough I'd be able to leave it all behind. Instead, it only worsened as fear blossomed in my chest.

On one hand, I reasoned, tonight could mark the beginning of the end. Dughall could get lucky and find everything we need to tie someone to this. We'd arrest them, figure out who they're working with, and get justice for everyone. On the other hand, it could go horribly wrong and put us back at square one leaving us unsure of where to go from here.

I stopped abruptly in the middle of the hallway, trying to shake away the negative thoughts. I was prepared for the worst-case scenario, but I needed to try to stay positive. That's the only way I was going to get through this with my sanity intact.

"Feyre?"

I looked up to see Merindah standing in front of me. Her eyebrows were scrunched together and her lips formed a slight frown.

"Yes?" I said. My voice sounded distant.

"I asked if you were alright," she said.

"Oh. Yeah," I said slowly. It took a moment for the gears in my head to start turning again. "I'm just trying to keep my mind off things is all. Waiting around for results is the worst part."

"I'm sure someone will find something soon," she said. Then she smiled. "It might even be the piece of the puzzle that we've been needing to solve all of this."

Her optimism was greatly appreciated. It made it easier for me to wrangle my negative thoughts and shove them into their box once more.

"I hope so. I'm already tired of this lockdown."

Merindah laughed. "We're on the same page there. I miss the hustle and bustle of Reidell."

"You, my dear, definitely have your priorities straight."

We said our goodbyes so she could get back to work. I decided that walking wasn't doing the trick. I needed something else to keep my mind preoccupied. I slowly made my way back to my bedroom to find something to hopefully keep me busy for the rest of the day.

~~~~~~~~~~~~~~~~

I fell asleep after dinner, setting an alarm for midnight. I'd been at the library for about an hour already, wide awake and circling the library anxiously. Up the stairs, around the second floor, down the stairs, zigzagging around the bookcases and tables on the first floor, then back up the stairs again. I'd been at it for what felt like an eternity as my brain swirled with every little thing that could go wrong tonight.

I started spiraling and this time I couldn't figure out how to stop it. My heart rate and breathing increased, so did my pace. I knew thanks to my earlier endeavor that I couldn't outrun these thoughts and feelings, but that wasn't going to stop me from trying.

Another half-hour had ticked by. I wasn't sure how much longer I could wait. I needed to know what was happening.

"Feyre!" Alliard shouted. "Are you in here?"

I weave through the bookcases and tables, making my way to the entrance of the library. Beside Alliard stood Dughall. He looked tired but unharmed. A large bag slung over his shoulder. A pit formed in my stomach as I stared at it.

"I slept in and by the time I was coming to join you, I saw some guards at the front doors looking a bit pissy. They were giving Dughall here a hard time about needing to speak with you so late, but I was able to get it all sorted out," Alliard explained.

Dughall grinned. "And I already thanked him for the rescue, so you don't need to give me that speech. I was even nice enough to use his name instead of calling him 'guard dog'"

"Never thought I'd see the day where you decided it was time to grow up, Dughall," I said.

He shrugged. "It has to happen eventually."

"Alright, enough small-talk. I need to hear what you have for me."

"From what I've heard, she's been pacing through the palace all day, so it'd probably be best to not argue with her," Alliard said.

"I get it, we're all dealing with a ticking time bomb here," Dughall said. "Just tell me where we're doing this."

I led them over to the couches. Alliard and I took one couch while Dughall and his bag took the other.

"We'll start with what I mentioned in the letter I sent to you this morning. I'm sure you've been dying to hear about it all day," Dughall said. He pulled out a stack of files from his bag and set them on the table. "I have files on a decent chunk of the missing people. I had my guys go around and pester whoever they worked for until they got something. They got descriptions, contacts, personal information like addresses, and any family members they might have. Some had fingerprints and DNA on file from previous crimes, so those are in there too if they had it. Most didn't, though, so don't get your hopes up."

"Hopefully our monster is one of these people, so we can try to match it," I said.

"That's your plan?" Alliard asked.

I nodded. "I know it's a long shot since we have no idea what the experimentation of transformation did to them, but it's worth a shot."

Alliard lightly jabbed his elbow into my ribs. "Thinking like a Queen already."

I gave him a small smile and turned my attention back to Dughall. I hoped he'd move onto the meeting next. That's what I really wanted to hear about.

Dughall puffed his cheeks out, blowing out a stream of air. "I'm going to start by saying I don't think you'll be happy with what I have to say next."

"I've spent all day preparing myself for every worst-case scenario imaginable, so I doubt whatever happened is as bad as what I've imagined," I laughed nervously.

He pulled out a small notebook from his bag and dropped it on top of the files. He leaned forward with his elbows on his knees.

"Alright. So. I brought along my shadow magic friend as a precaution, though I was able to get through the barrier without him. There were about twenty people there. I got their names and descriptions, all are in the notebook. I tried to get everything down to their last freckle for you. Now, we had a bit of time before our host arrived to mingle and introduce ourselves. Most of who showed up had to be new to the criminal lifestyle because they were quick to brag. They were also all rich. All powerful. They would have no problem providing people."

"So he sent more invites to lesser-known organizations and people this time," Alliard said.

"That's what it seems like," Dughall replied. "After what felt like forever, our host finally graced us with his presence. Here's where you're going to be disappointed. It wasn't Drystan. Looked nothing like him."

"I thought people were going around describing Drystan to a T," I said.

Dughall nodded. "They were."

"Illusion magic isn't a hard thing to do on yourself," Alliard pointed out."

"That's what my friend and I were thinking. That's where my last piece of evidence comes into play," Dughall said. He pulled out a plastic bag and dropped it on top of the pile. "At the very end of the meeting, we were getting ready to leave. I made my way over and blew smoke up his ass. I thanked him for the invite and promised him I'd talk to my guys about working for him. While I had him distracted, my friend plucked some hairs off his head so you guys could run a DNA test."

"So we have a fifty-fifty shot right now," I sighed.

"I know this isn't what you were hoping to hear, but I can't make evidence just appear," Dughall said.

I shook my head. "No, no. You did what you could, which is all we can ask for."

"I'll keep an ear out over the next few days to see if anyone says anything helpful."

"Thank you," I said. "I'll contact Eos first thing in the morning. As soon as I know anything, I'll contact you."

We said our goodbyes and Dughall made his way out of the palace. Alliard and I remained in the library. We stayed silent avoiding each other's gaze. We abruptly stood up, facing each other, both our mouths open. Looking at each other, we snapped our mouths shut. We did this a few times before awkwardly looking away from each other.

"I…uh…I should get back to the barracks. All the training and exercising I did today has me exhausted and sore," Alliard said.

"Uh. Yeah. Right. I should probably get some sleep too. I want to contact Eos as early as I can so she can run the DNA and see if she can identify our creature," I replied.

We awkwardly made our way out of the library together. Once outside, he veered to the left toward the backdoor and to the barracks. I went in the opposite direction toward the grand staircase. I stood at the bottom of the staircase, watching him walk away, feeling stupid.

"Real smooth, Feyre," I whispered to myself.

I made my way up the stairs forcing myself to focus on more important matters. There was one big thing I couldn't help but

20.

wonder about — when was the next attack going to happen?

Even with the lockdown, it could only be a matter of time. It might not be a giant massacre. It might not be a Royal getting attacked. It could be a destroyed building. A guard harmed on patrol. It could be a forest set ablaze. It could be anything.

I had a terrible feeling that something was going to happen. As much as I tried to push away the feeling of dread, that pit in my stomach refused to budge. All I could do was hope and pray that I was wrong.

21.

I spent the remaining early hours tossing and turning in bed, unable to fall asleep. The sun had begun to rise, so I gave up on sleeping entirely. I got out of bed quickly and began my usual morning routine. I was headed toward my closet, but stopped when my eyes locked with the pile of evidence.

I wanted to contact Eos right this second and hand over everything. I couldn't, though. She wouldn't be awake right now and I'd feel awful if I woke her up. With a small sigh, I forced myself into my closet to get dressed for the day.

I pulled my pants on, thinking about how I could pass the time. I couldn't fathom being in the palace any longer. I didn't want to wander through the same halls and rooms for the umpteenth time. I wanted to be outside enjoying the fresh air. I decided that a walk through Reidell was in order.

My parents weren't awake yet. They couldn't stop me. The guards would look at me strangely, but I know they wouldn't stop me. With all the guards patrolling I'd have assistance if I was attacked. There was nothing to worry about. I hoped.

I finished getting dressed, threw my hair up in a messy bun, and made my way downstairs. I hesitated as my hand wrapped around the doorknob of the front door. I took a deep breath, then pushed it open, stepping into the outside world. The guards sent a few glances my way as I walked down the steps, but no one made a move to stop me as I walked through the front gates.

I was free.

My eyes drifted to the world around me as I walked down the empty sidewalks. All shops, cafes, boutiques, stalls, and restaurants were closed. There wasn't anyone dragging themselves to work. No one was wrangling exhausted children to daycare. No one was shouting out the latest newspaper headlines. The only thing around were the guards in their new armor with their new weapons strapped to them. Their preparedness to attack at any second only added to the fear and tension that already hung in the air.

Without the usual hustle and bustle, it didn't take long to reach downtown. Seeing the park was another shock. This place was never empty. Not even this early in the morning. People were usually here enjoying their coffee, tea, or breakfast before work. Some would be reading their morning newspaper. Others would be getting in their morning exercise.

It was a ghost town.

I made my way to the dorioya tree and hoisted myself up onto the planter. This tree was a bit bigger than the one at the academy. Its glow was that much more magnificent. It shone so brightly no street lights were needed.

My eyes drifted closed as I drew in a deep breath of fresh morning air. The light breeze made me feel the most relaxed I'd felt in days.

"Nice to see you alive, Feyre."

My eyes snapped open as I crafted a sword in my hand.

Drystan's eyed my sword. "I didn't mean to startle you."

I let it disappear, but I kept my guard up. My eyes moved over him, acknowledging that he was dressed in a nice suit.

"What are you doing here?" I asked.

He tilted his head ever so slightly. "Do I need a reason to come visit a friend?"

"Considering you've never called us friends before, yes. Yes, you do."

"We've been friends since I became heir. At least, that's what I always thought."

With a growing sense of unease, my eyes darted around the park, easily spotting the surrounding guards. There were a good handful close enough to jump in. Drystan laughed abruptly when he noticed my discomfort.

"They can't see us, Feyre. We're in our own little bubble," he said. "Besides, I'm not here to hurt you. I just want to talk."

Shadow magic. Something easily broken by aether. I wasn't defenseless here.

"Then talk," I said, my voice emotionless.

"A little birdy told me you have people keeping an eye on me."

"Now why would this little birdy say such a thing?" I asked. "I'm but a simple Princess doing her best to help her country during a troubled time. Spying on someone — someone who's supposed to be a colleague, might I add — wouldn't be very queenly would it?"

Drystan narrowed his eyes. "Cut the bullshit Feyre. What do you know?"

I leaned forward, resting my chin in my hand. "What do I know about *what* exactly?"

He took a few quick steps forward closing the distance between us. I saw the fury blazing in his eyes. He looked as if he were begging me to give him an excuse to lash out.

"Stop playing dumb with me and tell me what the hell you know," he growled.

Technically, I didn't know anything. But he didn't know that. This would be my one opportunity to get something out of him, though.

Keeping my face and voice calm, I said, "I know you're behind the creation of these creatures. And getting the humans you turn into them. I know you've had to do some serious experimentation on humans to get to this point and clearly you've perfected it. You're obviously creating some sort of army with them for some big finale."

"Is that all you know?" he asked.

I shrugged. "Perhaps."

"You already know I'm not I'm not someone to mess with, so I suggest you stop fucking with me and tell me what I want to know."

"You aren't as scary as you think you are, Drystan."

A sly smile settled on his face. It put me more on edge.

"Oh really?"

I met his eyes and said, "You're a coward hiding behind monsters that you send out to do your bidding." I let out a breathy laugh. "I mean, how often have you been around me since you started this disaster? You could have simply killed me yourself and instead you waited until I was away from Reidell in some small, obscure town. Though, I guess I should have expected that, considering before this, you hid behind Morana's skirts like a terrified child."

He did this. He was behind this.

Drystan let out a dark laugh as he shook his head. "Just you wait, Feyre. Just you wait."

With that, he was gone. I stared at the spot where he'd been standing as I pushed out a shaky breath. I was wrong. I was all wrong. I needed to tell my parents. I needed to tell Eos.

I jumped off the planter, slipped off my flats, and bolted towards the palace. It didn't take long for me to get back. When I did get back, so did the guards. It was time for the morning shift change.

I elbowed my way through the crowd, getting jostled as I did. After too long, a couple of guards realized who I was and parted the crowd so I could get through. I rushed up the steps of the palace. Luckily, I spotted Merindah as I was running past the staircase.

"Are my parents awake yet?" I asked frantically.

A look of confusion washed over her face. "Yes. They told me to come get you, but you weren't in your room so I was coming to look for you in the library. You're needed in the War Room."

My eyes widened, my fear spiking. "Was there another attack?"

He couldn't work that quickly...could he?

"I don't know. Calla told me to come get you and get you down to the War Room. She didn't seem panicked or worried," she answered. "Are you alright, dear?"

"I don't have time to explain, just make sure the guard change happens quickly and tell them to be on their A-game."

"Feyre—"

I didn't hear anything else she said because I was already running towards the basement steps. I was still in motion when I cut my finger, causing a few drops of blood to hit the floor. I swiped my finger across the door and it opened painfully slowly. I stuffed my feet back into my flats while shifting my weight between my feet anxiously. When it opened, it revealed all of Council, Mother, and Eos sitting at the round table. Drystan was nowhere to be seen.

"We were worried you wouldn't make it," Demir said as I walked in.

"Are you alright, Fey?" Mother asked. "You looked flushed."

I waved her off. "Please tell me there wasn't another attack."

"There wasn't," Eos said. "What's happening is arguably worse."

"Do we have time to fill her in, or should we wait until we arrive?" Father asked.

Where were we going if there wasn't another attack?

"Best to fill her in now. We'll need her prepared, focused, and ready to work," Eos answered.

Before I could let loose a barrage of questions, Amara began talking.

"You know about Moroluma's history, correct?"

I nodded. "It's basic history we learn in what feels like every year in academy."

"The wards are failing and the dark energy is spreading," Amara stated.

"How?" I asked.

"We don't know," Mother said.

"Maintenance and strength tests were just done a month ago. I have no idea how this could have happened," Morana said. She sounded panicked, which is odd for her.

"It started last night," Amara said, capturing my attention again. "I went to speak with Morana about mine and Eos' latest finding to see if she could help us. As I was leaving Moroluma, I noticed the darkness appeared like it had extended past the wards. I thought maybe it was a trick of the light or something.

I put a marker down and had someone go out and check this morning. The dark energy was indeed spreading."

"I had someone run tests on the wards this morning, and they are weaker than they should be. Amara sent people to attempt to repair them while we both called this meeting," Morana said.

"The other Elders are working on creating wards around Felluna as it's the closest Kingdom to Moroluma putting it at the greatest risk," Eos said. "Another aether user would be helpful."

I bit the inside of my cheek. I needed to tell them about Drystan as soon as possible, but this took priority. If the wards shattered, all of Etrayus was at risk. Not just Felluna. We'd deal with this, then I'd tell them everything.

"I'll help as much as I can," I said firmly.

Eos grinned. "Wonderful."

"We should get out there then. The sooner these new wards are up the better we'll all feel," Mother said.

Amara was the first one on her feet. She created the portal. A line formed as everyone stepped through one by one, but Eos hung back with me.

"Do we have the evidence?" she asked once we were alone.

"It's in my room, but things have escalated since last night," I answered.

Eos nodded. "As soon as we deal with this, we'll talk about everything and decide where to go from there."

22.

It was clear to see that it was all hands on deck when we stepped through the portal into Felluna. The Elders were working on crafting the new wards while a few others ran tests to gauge their strength. Amara's right-hand man ran over to Eos and I. His eyes were wide and I swear I could see him trembling.

"Thank god you're here. You two are needed at the Moroluma wards immediately. The dark energy is starting to spread quicker and it's already undone the cleansing!"

"Have you sent anyone there to start cleansing?" I asked.

He shook his head. "We just got word. Queen Amara said to send you people out there immediately, I just happened to run into you first."

"Send as many people as you can help. It's going to take a lot to cleanse the land and keep it that way," I instructed.

"Yes, Princess," he said before scurrying off.

"I'm going to go check in with the other Elder and then I'll be there to supervise and help," Eos said.

She left me to craft a portal to Moroluma. I stepped through the portal and saw that the dark energy had spread a few feet past the wards. Everyone worked frantically on the repairs. It was impossible to miss their nervous eyes darting to the ground every few seconds.

I took a deep breath to calm my own nerves.

"Keep focusing on the repairs," I ordered. "I'm going to try to force the energy back to the ward line. There are others on the way to help. Elder Eos will also be joining us to assist."

I dropped to my knees in front of the dark energy. I pressed my hands into the ground letting my aether flow into the land. At first, I could feel the darkness fighting against me, trying to force me and my aether away. I forced more of my magic into the earth, keeping it at bay. For now.

It wasn't long before I heard a portal open followed by shuffling behind me. I saw a group of familiar faces coming out of the portal when I looked over my shoulder. There were about ten or fifteen people. The last to step out was Eos. She gave me a small smile and made her way over to one of the people doing repairs.

The newcomers spaced themselves a few apart from one another and sat on the ground like I was. They began feeding their magic into the land. When I felt their power in the land alongside mine, I decreased the amount of magic I was using. I felt relieved to be able to relax a bit.

It wasn't long before we were able to force the dark energy to retreat. Soon enough we'd pushed it back behind the wards. We kept our hands right outside the ward's edge to ensure the dark energy wouldn't be able to spread past them.

"Where are we at with the repairs?" I asked.

"They still need a bit more time. Things are taking longer than expected because the energy is more powerful than it should be," Eos answered.

Everyone shifted into a more comfortable sitting position as we glanced at one another. We were in it for the long haul. I wasn't sure how long we'd be able to keep this up which made me nervous.

When close to an hour has passed, I felt myself growing exhausted. I felt drained and it was getting harder to keep myself sitting up straight. Looking around, I could see others starting to slump forward or their eyes fluttering as they tried to keep them open. None of us spoke up or complained. We did our best to push on.

Ten minutes. Twenty minutes. Thirty minutes. Time was passing quickly, but it felt like there was no actual progress being made.

"Is there any way to speed this up?" someone shouted.

"Repairing these wards isn't exactly easy!" a woman shouted back.

"We're going as quickly as we can!"

"Everyone quiet down and focus!" Eos shouted. "That's the only way this is going to work!"

No one protested further. We returned our focus to the task at hand, keeping our magic steady and stable. Another few minutes passed and something felt...off.

At first, I was convinced I was imagining it, but then I felt it again. I wasn't sure how to describe it. It wasn't like earlier when I felt the energy bucking and fighting against me. It was almost as if it was...swelling?

"Is anyone else feeling this?" I shouted.

I got a chorus of 'I feel it too' or 'what the hell is happening?' in response.

"What's happening, Feyre?" Eos asked urgently.

I shook my head and my heart started pounding. "I have no idea!"

"I'd suggest you guys hurry up with these damn repairs,

though!" someone shouted.

"I'm gonna have to second that! Whatever this is, it can't be good!"

"Everyone! Keep your focus and release as much magic as you can!" I ordered.

"Give them a couple more minutes and the wards should be back to their usual power levels!" Eos shouted.

I felt a surge of power around me as we poured our magic into the earth. The odd feeling began to fade. I felt a sense of relief as some tension left me.

A short-lived reprieve.

In the blink of an eye, a large burst of energy threw everyone away from the wards. It felt like I got hit by a truck. I slammed into the ground a few feet away, watching in horror as the wards exploded. Glittery shards rained down across the grass as the dark energy began spreading and infecting the land beneath us. It was spreading too quickly for us to stop it. We could do nothing but watch as it sped toward Felluna. Toward the rest of Etrayus.

"Everyone to Felluna! Now!" Eos ordered.

I pulled my eyes away from the ground to see that she had already created a portal. No one moved for a few minutes, taking time to process what was happening. It hit us all at once. We scrambled to our feet rushing through the portal as quickly as we could. I silently prayed that Felluna's wards would be strong enough to withstand this.

I burst through the portal, my heart moving into my throat. I dropped to my knees when I saw the wards were still, thankfully, holding strong.

"They tried their hardest," Eos said, shaking her head.

"I know they did, but sometimes our hardest isn't enough,"

Amara said.

"What do we do about the rest of Etrayus? Is there even anything we can do?" Demir asked.

"Felluna is protected and Dradour should be fine for now since it's in the mountains. Artheas and Reidell though, they're at risk. Based on the rate that this is spreading, we won't have time to set up wards powerful enough to guarantee their protection," Eos said.

My mother went into a visible panic. I could see her chest falling and rising quickly as her face grew flushed. Amara and Csilla sat her down on a nearby stump, speaking quietly but quickly in an attempt to calm her down. Father and Demir remained stone-faced. All the Elders looked conflicted. Everyone on Amara's team looked pale and looked like they were going to vomit.

I was pissed and terrified. Drystan and whoever was working with him were doing this. They were destroying my home. They were hurting innocent people that we were supposed to vow to protect.

Morana, though. She looked heartbroken. Maybe even a little guilty. A strange sight given that she rarely showed any emotions. She always hid behind her overconfidence and smugness.

"I should have been keeping a closer eye on the wards," Morana said.

"You did the yearly tests and maintenance. That's all anyone expects you to do," Father said.

"I should have noticed something was wrong before Amara did!" she screeched. "This is my Kingdom! Those are my wards! They're my responsibility and I let them fail!"

"Morana," Demir said calmly. "I know we haven't always

gotten along or seen eye to eye, but trust me when I say this. None of us blame you. Zander's right. You do what we expect of you. You couldn't have known this was going to happen or even known this was a possibility. We've never had a problem with the wards before."

"There's no point in blaming ourselves or pointing fingers. What's done is done. All we can do now is try to figure out a solution to our current problem," Father stated. He then turned to Eos. "Elder Eos, what should we do?"

"Three Elders go to Artheas. One and myself will go to Reidell. Council and Felluna's teams split up as well. We might not have time to create the wards we need, but that doesn't mean we shouldn't try," Eos answered.

"Does everyone have enough energy for this?" Amara asked her teams.

Whether or not they were lying, everyone said they were fine to keep going.

"Feyre, can you create wards?" Eos asked.

"Basic ones at best," I answered.

"Well, I hope you're a quick learner because we need all hands on deck."

We all had our assignments, which helped everyone regain their composure. Morana had gone back to her usual emotionless self and Mother had gotten herself under control. Amara, Morana, and Csilla would go to Artheas. Mother, Father, Demir, and I would return to Reidell. Once that was decided, Amara split her teams in half while the Elders spoke amongst themselves to decide where they'd go.

We shared a few words of encouragement as a pair of portals were created. We wished each other luck, then went our separate ways.

23.

We were able to get back to Reidell before the dark energy had a chance to spread that far. The Elders, Mother, and I quickly got to work on building wards while Father and Demir spoke with the guards and palace staff. We needed all the help we could get.

Eos stood next to me talking me through the process of creating wards this large and powerful. She was extremely patient with me. If I needed her to reexplain something, she would. If I had any questions, she'd answer them without hesitation. It made me wish she would have been one of my teachers at the academy.

We were able to get the foundation of the wards up by the time Father and Demir had returned. They were able to gather around thirty people, including Alliard. We were on opposite ends, making it easier to not get distracted by one another.

Thanks to the number of people we had, we were able to strengthen the wards with ease. I hoped they were having the same luck in Artheas. I didn't want to think about what would happen if we lost Artheas to this. It would be detrimental to Etrayus.

A long hour later, we all had to watch with bated breath as the dark energy rushed towards us. It took every ounce of power to focus on continuing to build the wards, hoping it would tip the scales in our favor.

It happened in slow motion. The small gap of land that was green and lush quickly became black and tainted. The dark energy slammed into the wards and everyone flinched back.

Nothing shattered.

We watched for a few tense minutes to see if that would change. It didn't. We were in the clear. The wards were holding strong. Our work wasn't done, however.

The Elders thought it would be best to go until we physically couldn't anymore. The wards needed to be as strong as we could possibly get them. So, that's what we did. We were able to work until the sun started to set. Most of our people began feeling winded, lightheaded, and drained. The Elders, and a few from Amara's team, tested the wards to see how powerful they were. They were more powerful than the ones around Felluna — a pleasant surprise.

Amara's team returned to Felluna. The guards and palace staff returned to their jobs. The Elders were getting ready to return to Artheas for the night, but Father invited them to join us for dinner. They happily agreed, so Mother and Father took them as well as Demir to a parlor to relax until dinner was ready. Eos, though, stayed behind so we could talk.

"I believe you and I have some things to go over," she said. "Would you like to speak in the War Room or would you prefer the library?"

"The library. I need somewhere comfortable to sit for a bit," I said, trying to hide just how exhausted I was.

I didn't need to lead the way this time, as Eos knew where she was going. I pulled aside a staff member asking them to bring us some tea and have someone bring me the files from my room.

23.

I joined Eos who was already getting herself comfortable on one of the couches. I took my seat across from her.

We only had to wait a few minutes before they served our tea. The files took a bit longer to get to us. Eos and I filled out time with small talk.

"You did great out there today," Eos said, pouring our tea.

"We all did," I responded. "I'll be honest. I thought we all would've collapsed before we could even think about creating wards around Reidell."

She smiled. "I'll admit, I did too. But I'm glad to see that Etrayus is still full of powerful people."

We grew quiet as we sipped on our tea. As we were each finishing up our first cup and started our second, a servant returned, holding all the evidence. She handed it off to me, then scurried off before I could thank her.

I set everything on the table and pushed it toward Eos. She picked up the files and started flipping through them. As she skimmed, I began talking. I recapped everything Dughall told me. Eos sat silently, nodding along to show she was listening.

"So, we're back to square one until we can get this hair tested or match that monster to one of these people," she said when I finished speaking.

"That's where Dughall's evidence ends," I said. "But I told you this morning that things had escalated."

"I think I already know I'm not going to like what you have to say, so please. Continue."

"I snuck out this morning to go for a walk. While I was in the park, a certain friend of ours decided to appear to me," I said.

Eos sat up a little straighter, leaned forward a bit, and looked me in the eye. "Drystan?"

I nodded, smiling. "Drystan. He found out that I had people following him. He became very upset and demanded to know what I knew. I told him our speculations. Based on his reactions, I'd say we hit the nail on the head," I said. "We exchanged a few…not so nice words after that and he ended it with 'just you wait, Feyre' before leaving."

"That sounds like a threat to me," Eos said.

"I'd like to tell my parents about this tonight. We need to figure out what we can do about him and we need to do it fast."

"I agree," Eos said.

Dinner would not be the relaxing event that everyone was expecting. All I could hope was that everyone would believe me so we could act quickly. If we waited, it gave Drystan more time to work on whatever he had planned.

Which could mean he'd have time to work on another attack.

Please god let them believe me.

~~~~~~~~~~~~~~~~

It was roughly an hour after our business conversations stopped that we were told dinner was ready. It wasn't prepared for the conversation that needed to be had, but there was no getting out of it.

Eos and I walked into the dining room together. At first, it appeared that we were the last to arrive. I scanned the room and saw that Mother wasn't there. I took my usual seat and Eos sat beside me. I listened to the idle chat, deciding to wait until dinner to speak up.

"Where's Mother?" I asked.

"She went to Felluna tonight. She wanted to see if she could help figure out why the wards failed and how to reverse what's been done. She also wants to run some tests to see if we need to evacuate all the towns and cities or if they'll be alright for now," Father answered.

"Did someone make an announcement telling the towns and cities what happened?"

He nodded. "I asked Csilla to send out memos to all the officials."

"Were they able to get the wards up in Artheas in time?" Eos asked.

"Barely," Demir answered.

That was a small relief. Our Kingdoms were safe, giving citizens a place to retreat if we needed to evacuate. I hoped it wouldn't come to that.

Dinner was served and everyone immediately dug in. I took a few bites of my salad, but that's all I could choke down. My appetite was nowhere to be found.

"I know who's behind the attacks!" I blurted.

My cheeks burned as everyone's eyes snapped over to me. I intended to tell them a bit more eloquently, but my anxiety betrayed me.

"What do you mean?" Father asked.

I cleared my throat. "Well, I know who's behind the creatures."

"And you're just now bringing this up?" Demir asked.

"I only found out this morning. I wanted to tell you all then, but the wards needed our attention and well...we all know what happened after that," I said. I hung my head, no longer able to look at any of them. I took a deep breath and said, "It's Drystan."

I lifted my head enough to see if I could gauge what responses I was going to get. The shock on Demir and Father's faces made it seem like I'd accused Mother of being behind this. I opened my mouth to start telling them everything, but they both spoke over me.

"We would've known it was him!"

"This is a mistake."

"He's been with us every step of the way!"

"Exactly! It would be impossible for him to do all of this! Especially without someone noticing!"

Eos interrupted them, "That is enough!"

Both fell quiet, their faces grew red. They looked like children who had just been scolded by their mothers.

"I've heard her evidence and explanations. I'm on her side with this. I'm sure if you hear her out, you'll be on her side too."

The Elders appeared emotionless. Demir and Father gave each other a glance before giving me their attention.

"Alright," Father said. "Tell us what you have."

Not wanting to endure them talking over me again, I disclosed everything I'd been hiding. I went through every detail we had, piecing everything together. They didn't look convinced until I spoke about my encounter this morning. Like Eos, they sat up a little straighter and clung onto my every word.

"You're one-hundred percent sure it was him this morning?" Demir asked.

"There's no doubt in my mind. It was him," I said firmly.

"And what of this hair Dughall got? When will it be tested?" Father asked.

"I'll be running a DNA test as soon as I return to Artheas tonight," Eos answered.

"How quickly can you get that done?"

"I can have the results by tomorrow evening," she replied.

It grew quiet. Then, Father nodded.

23.

"I'd like to wait until we get the results," Father said. I opened my mouth to object, but he raised a hand, stopping me. "I'm not saying that I don't believe you, because I do. I just want to have the evidence in hand before we alert Council and arrest Drystan publicly."

"I'd suggest telling Morana separately as a courtesy. Today rattled her. There's no telling what this will do to her," Demir said.

"We'll decide what to do next once we have the results," Father said.

"As soon as I have them, I'll bring them directly to you," Eos stated.

Father leaned back into his chair looking exhausted. "It doesn't matter the time of day or what I might be doing; bring them directly to me. We need to get this whole thing taken care of immediately. I don't want to give Drystan and whoever he's working with to bring anymore harm to Etrayus."

Hope swelling inside me.

One more day. One more day and this whole nightmare would be over.

24.

Everything was already in place for this evening. If the DNA came back confirming it was Drystan, we wouldn't need to scramble for a plan. Mother, Amara, and Csilla were filled in on the new information this morning. All armies had been informed of what was happening, so they were prepared if the worst came to pass.

Csilla was working on trying to confirm if our creature matched one of the missing people. Amara had sent people out to put more wards around the dorioya trees. She'd also send people to put wards around cities and towns.

While the darkness had already spread, we hoped we'd be able to cleanse the land quickly to avoid any long-term damage.

We also already had a plan in place to get Morana and Drystan here. Father was going to tell them he and Mother wanted to discuss options about healing Etrayus and building new wards around Moroluma. Morana would talk with Mother, Father, and Eos in the office while I would go into a parlor with Drystan. We'd give them time to discuss what was really happening and guards would rush into the parlor to arrest Drystan. He'd be safely transported to prison where he'd be questioned and pressed for information about who he was working with. Or, perhaps, even for.

24.

I'd been in the library for most of the day trying to distract myself with books as time slowly ticked by. It was evening now. Eos could be here any time now with the results.

"Feyre?" Alliard's voice rang out. "Are you in here?"

Anxiety and panic consumed me. We hadn't spoken since that night he came to my room. I'd seen him around the palace on duty, but I did my best to avoid him.

My first instinct was to ignore him and hope he left. When I heard his footsteps echoing around the library I knew it was a lost cause. He was looking for me. If he spotted me here, then he'd known I'd ignored him. That would only make things that much more awkward.

Letting out a small sigh, I shouted, "Up here!"

The footsteps stopped for half a second. Then I heard them coming up the stairs. A moment later, he stood in front of me.

"I think it's about time we talked," he said.

"Oh?" I said, laughing nervously. "Is everything okay?"

"I don't know," he responded. "You keep dodging me."

I scoffed. "I'm not dodging you."

"Well, either way, I'd like to talk to you about something," he said. "About us, to be specific."

If my heart wasn't already racing, that would have sent it galloping. I tried to reply, but the words got stuck in my throat leaving me with my mouth open. Alliard didn't seem to care as he continued to speak.

"King Zander already warned us about everything that could happen today. If things go horribly wrong, I don't want to go down without you knowing how I feel about you or how you feel about me."

There really was no avoiding this conversation. I wanted to hear what he had to say, but at the same time, I didn't. I'd convinced myself that I'd been misinterpreting everything that was happening between us. He had to be here to confirm that and let me down easy. He might even call me his little sister or best friend. The thought of that made me want to throw up and start crying.

I didn't want to be his little sister or his best friend.

"O-okay," I stuttered.

Alliard took my stammering as an invitation to sit across from me in the window seat. We were facing each other but I refused to meet his gaze. I wasn't ready for this. I felt sick.

"I need you to look at me if we're going to do this," Alliard whispered. "Please."

Digging my fingernails into my palms, I forced myself to meet his eyes. As soon as our gazes locked, neither of us could look away, even though I desperately wanted to.

"I like you Feyre," he said. He sounded as if he'd rehearsed this a million times. "And not just as family or friends. I like you more than some lowly guard should like a beautiful Princess. I know it's wrong. I know nothing can happen between us. But I couldn't go into tonight without telling you how I felt."

The pile of imaginary bricks crushing me vanished at his words. He *liked* me. He liked me in the way that I liked him! I hadn't been imagining all of this. I hadn't missed all the hints and signs or misinterpreted anything. He liked me.

"Alliard—"

"I know, I know. You don't have to let me down easy."

"Alliard I—"

"Just rip it off like a bandage."

"I—"

"I understand. You don't have to feel bad."

"Alliard!" I shouted.

24.

He blinked at me, startled out of his rambling. "Yes?"

I laughed, shaking my head. "Can I talk now?"

"Please do," he said, his cheeks glowing red.

"I like you," I said, smiling. "Not as friends or family. More than a Princess should like her guard. No, it isn't wrong and something definitely can happen between us."

I didn't realize how great it would feel to say it out loud. I didn't realize how great it would feel to hear him say it to me. I was on cloud nine.

"Wait," he said, a smile growing on his face. "Can you repeat that again? I don't think I heard you."

"I like you and definitely not in a friend way."

He grinned. "And the other thing?"

I rolled my eyes, still smiling. "It isn't wrong and something can definitely happen between us."

Alliard quickly reached out and pulled me closer to him. His eyes flicked down to my lips. Unlike that night in my room, there was no hesitation. No stopping himself. He gently grabbed my chin, then pressed his lips to mine. I melted into his arms, kissing him back. It was the best kiss I'd ever gotten. After a few seconds, we pulled away from one another.

"I will now forever be pissed that I didn't do that last time," he said, laughing.

"You and me both," I laughed with him. "So I'll take this as we're like…official."

Alliard shrugged. "You said it, not me."

I moved so I was straddling his lap. I took his face in my hands and kissed him again. And again. And then again. He put his hands on my hips and kissed me back.

"Does this mean you have to go run off and tell all your best friends about me? Or is this where you tell me we have to sneak around so that no one will ever know we're together?" he asked.

"Neither," I answered. "Everyone can find out on their own. Word about these things always spreads quickly."

He opened his mouth to respond but was cut off by Merindah calling from downstairs. "Feyre! Eos is here! She and your parents are waiting for you in the office!"

"Thank you! I'll head there now!" I called back. I looked at Alliard. "Care to join me for the final meeting about this disaster?"

He grinned. "I would be honored."

Hand in hand, we walked to my parents' office. A few guards saw and didn't bother trying to hide their smiles. When we reached the office door, Alliard tried to slip his hand out of mine, but I held on tightly.

"They'll hear all your friends gossiping in no time anyway, so there's no point in trying to hide it now," I whispered.

"But are you alright with them knowing?" he asked.

"Why wouldn't I be?"

Before he could respond, I stepped into the office pulling him with me. They noticed our intertwined fingers near-immediately.

An enormous smile took over Mother's face. "I'm glad to see you here, Alliard."

Father looked more sick than happy. "Alliard. Seems we need to have a conversation of our own when this is all over."

I rolled my eyes. "You say that like I've never had a boyfriend before."

"I've never liked any of them, so they might as well have not existed at all," Father said with a shrug. "Alliard through. I respect him."

24.

"Welcome to the royal family, Alliard," Eos said. Her grin matched Mother's though it fell quickly, morphing into something more serious. "As much as I'm sure we would all love to celebrate you two, we do have some business to attend to."

"Please tell me that hair was Drystan's," I said.

She paused for a moment, keeping her face emotionless. A knot formed in my stomach as my heart pounded. Then, a grin returned to her face. This one was bigger than the last.

"It is without a single doubt Drystan's hair," she said. "I had the other Elders and Csilla look at my results to make sure my old eyes weren't reading it wrong and they all agreed."

"What about that creature?" Mother asked.

"Csilla thinks she's matched it to one of the missing people based on scars, tattoos, and facial markers. A few others on her team agree with her findings. However, that could be a bit more questionable in a trial," Eos said.

"Well, it's good enough for me," Father said. "Alliard, go tell the guards to prepare. Feyre and Eos, I need you two to get word to Demir, Amara, and Csilla to prepare their armies and get Morana and Drystan here," Father ordered.

"Yes, sir," Alliard said.

"I'll contact Morana and Drystan. You get work to Amara, Demir, and Csilla," Eos said.

I nodded. "Sounds good."

"And Alliard, one more thing. I want you inside that parlor with Drystan and Feyre. You'll let the guards in and keep Feyre out of harm's way."

"Of course," Alliard said firmly. He pressed a quick kiss to my temple before rushing off to follow his orders.

"Within a few minutes, I had three aether birds sent off and

Eos had gotten one sent to Morana. Everyone in the office stood around impatiently awaiting a response.

An eternity later, Eos' bird returned with a letter from Morana saying that they would be here within the next ten minutes.

was the beginning of the end.

25.

I was standing around the corner at the top of the staircase. Neither Morana nor Drystan would be able to see me when they portaled in. My instructions were to wait here until someone called me down, then I'd go down to greet them. I'd take Drystan to a parlor upstairs and keep him occupied for a bit. Alliard would let the guards in and they'd handle Drystan.

Alliard gripped my hand tightly, giving away the fear flowing through his body.

"There's nothing to worry about," I said. "There are guards stationed in every nook and cranny throughout Reidell, so even if something goes wrong, there's no way he's walking out of here a free man."

"He managed to do all of this with no one knowing, so who's to say that he doesn't know exactly what he's about to walk into. For all we know, he could come in here with an army of those monsters following behind him."

"He can't do that, he's coming with Morana."

Alliard wrapped his hand around the back of my neck, pulling me in for a quick kiss.

"Feyre! Can you come down here please!" Mother shouted. That was my cue.

"Remember, you just need to keep him occupied for a few minutes, then we'll arrest him," Alliard said.

Taking a deep breath to calm my nerves, I nodded. A few minutes. I could do that.

We exchanged one more kiss before I rounded the corner and headed downstairs. Alliard was only a step or two behind me, dressed in his new armor and an aether sword I enchanted for him.

"Drystan, Morana," I said. "What are you doing here?"

"Your parents and Elder Eos want to discuss our options for cleansing the land and replacing the wards around Moroluma. I've read through a few books, and I think I might have found a cleansing ritual we can perform," Morana answered.

"That doesn't explain why I'm needed, though."

"We've asked Drystan to sit this one out. We were hoping that you would keep him company for a bit while we talk," Mother said.

"Yeah. I can do that," I said, nodding. I looked over at Drystan. "We'll go to one of the upstairs parlors. It's quieter up there."

Drystan let out an aggravated sigh. "Very well."

I said goodbye to the group and led Drystan upstairs. On the way up, I stopped a servant asking them to bring us some tea and pastries.

"I'm not having a tea party with you," Drystan said flatly.

I shrugged. "More for me then."

I stopped at the parlor door. Drystan shouldered past me and stepped inside the parlor without waiting for me. Alliard, who was already on edge, balled his hands into fists. My fingers grazed his knuckles as I gave him a quick smile. I followed Drystan inside and sat on the couch across from the chair Drystan had sat down in. Alliard took his post by the door, removing all emotion from his face.

"Why is he here?" Drystan asked, eyeing him. "I mean, he almost died and almost got you killed. That doesn't seem like someone who can be trusted to protect you."

"I got hurt because of my own stupidity. It had nothing to do with him," I stated.

Drystan snorted. "You keep telling yourself that."

"Does it always have to be like this when we're stuck together? Can't we at least pretend to like each other?"

"And here I was thinking that you loved our banter," he said, feigning hurt.

I rolled my eyes. "I never understood why you felt the need to put everyone else down to raise yourself up."

"I *earned* my spot as an heir. I *earned* the right to rule over Moroluma. You and all your pathetic royal friends get it handed to you all because you were born," he hissed. "I don't see it as putting you down. It's more like I'm putting you in your rightful places."

"Just because you 'earned' it doesn't automatically make you better than everyone else."

"Of course it does."

A couple of servants entered the room and interrupted our conversation. One carried in a tea tray while the other carried in a few plates of pastries and sweets. Drystan didn't acknowledge them. I thanked them as they left and poured myself a cup of tea.

"Alliard, feel free to help yourself," I said, picking up a mini tea cake. "God knows I can't eat all of this myself."

"Thank you, Princess," Alliard said. He stepped forward and took a couple mini tea cakes of his own before returning to his spot.

Drystan poured himself some tea. "Did your parents really call us here to discuss land cleansing?"

"They want to figure out a way to do it without also cleansing Moroluma," I answered.

He smirked. "So they do respect our history."

"Of course they do."

"See. I don't think I believe that."

My heart started racing as I glanced over at Alliard. He was moving toward the door. I shot him a sharp look and he stopped in his tracks. Drystan was already on edge. I didn't want to risk setting him off.

"Always so paranoid," I sighed, shaking my head.

"I have every reason to be paranoid here!" he snapped.

"Why is that?" I asked innocently.

His eyes darted over to Alliard. "Is your precious little guard over here the one who'd been watching me? I bet he is."

"He isn't."

"You know more than you let on the other day, don't you?"

I shrugged. "Of course I do."

Drystan chuckled. "Maybe you are smarter than you look."

"You really know how to make a girl feel special," I said flatly.

"Level with me Feyre," he said. "We both know you won't make it far into your Queen-hood alone. Your parents have to know this too and will probably want you married before they hand the throne over to you." He leaned forward a bit, looking me in the eyes. "I'll give up everyone I've worked with, all of our research and experimentation, and all of our future plants if you can guarantee me a place on Reidell's throne."

"Someone like you doesn't deserve to sit on a throne."

"Wrong an—"

He was interrupted by guards rushing into the room. Their

25.

armor made their steps louder and more intimidating.

"What the hell are you doing?" Drystan shouted.

They gripped his upper arms and hauled him to his feet. I heard the handcuffs lock around his wrists and felt relief flood my system.

"Tell me what you did to Moroluma's land and maybe I can get you a deal," I said.

"I prayed to the right God."

"Did Morana know what you were up to?"

"Princess, we really need to get him out of here," One guard said.

"Morana is as blind as the rest of you," Drystan stated. His eyes betrayed him, though. He looked terrified.

"Thank you for your help, Drystan," I said, coldly. I looked at the guards. "Get him out of here."

They didn't hesitate to drag him out. Drystan struggled and tried moving his hands to perform some sort of magic. Thanks to the enchantment on the handcuffs, though, he couldn't.

"We need to get down to the office. As soon as Morana hears he's been arrested, it's going to be game over for all of us," I said, frantically.

"What do you mean?" Alliard asked.

"Morana is part of this."

"How do you know?"

"He never leaves her side. He doesn't do anything without her explicit permission," I explained. "There's no way he got away with all of this without her knowing."

"That doesn't mean she's part of this. She could be protecting him."

I shook my head. "Morana loves power. She loves ruling over people and being in charge and being worshiped. She wouldn't be able to stand by letting Drystan get all this attention. She'd want in on it."

"That is one gigantic leap," Alliard said.

"Then take the lead of faith and trust me on this one. Please," I pleaded.

He looked conflicted but quickly relented. "Alright. Let's go."

26.

Everything appeared normal when we stepped out of the parlor. Nothing looked different or seemed out of place. Things were quiet at first. Then I heard a familiar growl. Alliard and I looked at each other for a moment then rushed over to the staircase. Those creatures, big and small, filled the entryway of the palace. The guards were battling them, doing their best to keep them away from the office door.

"Looks like we're going to have to fight our way through," I said.

We bolted down the stairs. As soon as our feet hit the marble floor, we joined the fight. We helped guards who were getting overwhelmed while creating a path for ourselves to the office. We each were able to take out a handful of creatures by the time we made it to the office door. I slipped inside while Alliard stayed to continue fighting.

My eyes searched the room quickly spotting Morana. She was sitting in a chair weeping while Mother tried to console her. Eos and Father looked sick.

"Feyre, what are you doing here? And what is all that noise out there?" Mother asked.

"She's in on it with him," I said, staring at Morana.

"What are you talking about?" Mother asked.

Morana's sobs turned to dark laughter. Her head snapped up and a proud smile took over her face.

"Bravo Feyre," Morana said. "Though, by the sounds that are coming from out there you're too late with this revelation."

She snapped her fingers and a portal opened up. Out stepped one of the larger creatures. The smell rolling off of it made me nauseous.

No one had time to react when it threw itself toward Mother. I raised my swords ready to kill it, but it was already too late. I watched as it slung its arm out. Its claws caught Mother's throat, ripping it open with ease. It was like scissors cutting through paper. As its arm dropped, its claws cut through Mother's chest stopping at her stomach. Blood poured down the front of Mother's now ripped dress, dripping down onto the rug underneath us.

I gripped my swords tighter and grit my teeth. I took two large steps forward, thrusting my swords into the creature's back. A horrendous roar filled the office making my eardrums throb. The creature flung its arms around frantically in an attempt to defend itself.

I ripped my swords out of its back already prepared to go for what would be the killing blow. Before I could, I was left watching in horror as its claws caught Father's stomach ripping it open with ease. He fell forward onto his desk, blood smearing over the papers that sat on it, then slumped to the ground with a *thump.*

My entire body froze. This couldn't be happening. This couldn't be happening!

I heard the sound of Morana's heels clicking against the floor. The office door opened and the sound quickly became distant until I couldn't hear them anymore.

An enraged scream left Eos. Her hand was radiating with aether as she pushed it into the creature's chest. When she ripped her hand out, the creature dropped to the floor next to Mother. Eos' hand was covered in thick, black blood and in her palm was the monster's heart.

My eyes drifted down to my mother's corpse. My body became wracked with sobs and I could feel my body trembling. I wrapped my arms around myself, stumbling back and dropping to my knees.

I silently begged Mother to make a noise or move. I begged Father to get up and do something. Neither of them did. Mother remained on the floor, her eyes wide looking up at the ceiling and her mouth open with a scream she didn't get out. I couldn't see Father from where I was, but I imagined him having the same look.

"Feyre? Feyre!"

Alliard.

"She's fine."

Eos.

I slowly blinked, coming out of my trance. My eyes darted around the room. Alliard was kneeling at my side while Eos remained standing, taking in the scene.

"They're…they're dead," I whispered.

No one spoke for a moment. I assumed they were processing what had happened like I was.

"Alliard, get the other guards and go after Morana and Drystan," Eos ordered, breaking the silence.

"No," I said, quickly.

I needed to pull myself together. I couldn't sit here sobbing like a child while the people who were responsible for this wandered freely through my home. I took my emotions locking them away into that little box, throwing it into the deepest part of my mind. My mind and body grew numb. I felt empty. But I was able to bring my focus back to the task at hand.

"Feyre—"

"No," I repeated. "I'm now the enacting Queen of Reidell. This is my call."

"Are you sure?" Eos asked.

"I've trained my entire life for this. I can do it," I answered. "I...I need to do this."

She nodded slowly. "Okay. Tell us what you want us to do."

"I need you to bring in reinforcements. We can handle things until you get back, but we won't get through this without more help."

"What are you going to do?" Eos asked, concerned.

"I'm going after Morana and Drystan. I will not let them roam Reidell without knowing what they're doing."

"I'll bring in reinforcements. Just please..." She glanced at Mother's body for a millisecond before returning her attention to me. "Be careful."

Eos still looked conflicted, but she didn't push the situation further. She opened a portal and stepped through it, vanishing.

With Alliard's help, I got to my feet. The first thing I saw when I was steady was the office door wide open. The guards in the entryway were standing there, staring. I bit my tongue holding in another round of sobs that wanted to come out and stepped out of the office to face them all. Alliard closed the door behind us blocking the scene from their view. No one else needed to see what happened in there.

The guards slowly shifted their attention to me. I didn't say anything at first. I was too busy looking around the entryway at the bodies of the creatures. Their blood was smeared all over the floor. Various pieces from them were scattered around. The only part of it that brought me joy was that none of the bodies on the ground were my guards. They all seemed unharmed.

"I need someone to bring Merindah to me now. I also need my cloak from my room," I ordered.

Two guards stepped away from the group and disappeared upstairs with no hesitation. I was grateful no one asked questions or questioned my authority. It made it easier to do this.

"I need a small group to stay with Alliard and I. The rest will need to get out there and begin clearing out any of the creatures in Reidell and get all citizens here to the palace. You'll take them to the basement and from there Merindah will be in charge of getting them out of here. Give these orders to any guards you see along the way," I said. "If you see Morana or Drystan, do not engage with them. Our top priority is to get as many people out of here as we can."

The group spoke amongst themselves deciding who would stay and who would go. It didn't take them long. Soon all but four guards had exited the palace and the two guards who'd disappeared upstairs had returned. One had Merindah in tow and the other was holding my cloak as if it were a child.

"Feyre, what's happening?" Merindah asked as she approached.

"We're under attack. I need you to go down to the basement and open the War Room. You remember where the blood vials are, right?"

She nodded. "Of course."

189

"Good. I'm going to have citizens brought down to the basement. From there, you'll bring them to the War Room and begin portaling them to Dradour," I instructed. Dradour was as far away from Reidell as you could get. In my head, that made it the safest option. "Keep everyone as calm as you can and when they start asking questions, keep your answers vague. I don't want anyone panicking while you're trying to get them out of here."

"What about—"

I shook my head, stopping her from asking. That seemed to be all she needed to understand what was happening. Tears began welling up in her eyes. Before any spilled over, she closed her eyes and took in a deep breath. When she opened her eyes, her features were stone-like.

"These two guards are going to stay with you. If you need anything at all, ask them and they'll do whatever you need them to."

"What are you going to do?" Merindah asked.

"I'm going after Morana and Drystan," I stated.

Surprisingly, it wasn't Merindah that protested. It was a guard.

"Shouldn't you go down to the War Room with her? As Queen of Reidell, you should be the first one out of here."

"I refuse to go run and hide someone while those two run around bringing ruin to my Kingdom."

She opened her mouth to argue further, but Alliard cut her off. "There's no point in trying to argue or reason with her. Once she's made up her mind, it would take a miracle to talk her out of it." Alliard turned his attention to the other guards. "And none of you worry, Feyre can hold her own in a fight. She isn't helpless. Treat her as you would any other guard; watch

26.

her back and jump in if you need to."

The girl nodded firmly. "Then lead the way, my Queen."

It was an odd thing to hear. I wasn't sure how I felt about it. I wasn't supposed to have that title until my parents decided I was ready for it. But that wouldn't happen now. It couldn't happen. I had to step up to the plate on my own.

Merindah pulled me into a tight hug and whispered, "Be careful Feyre. Come back to me in one piece."

"I will. I promise," I whispered back.

She took my cloak from the guard and put it on me. She latched the lotus at my neck, kissed me on the cheek, and began walking away with the two guards following her. I quickly wiped away a stray tear that had fallen and turned my attention to my small group.

"We will not be arresting Morana and Drystan. Our mission is to kill them. They've lost any rights to mercy or respect, so don't go easy on them because of their status," I said firmly.

"Yes, my Queen," everyone said in unison.

I rolled my shoulders back, kept my head up high, and walked toward the front doors. I formed my aether swords in my hands as Alliard pushed open the doors.

I knew the outside world would be something straight out of a nightmare. But what we were greeted with was far worse than I had imagined.

27.

Everything was dead. Except it wasn't just trees, grass, flowers, and shrubbery. There were birds, squirrels, and butterflies lying dead on the ground. Black masses drifted through the air around us and the sky was pitch black as if it were the middle of the night. However, based on the time, the sun should still be setting. The street lanterns were lit, but dim. The glass that encased the bulbs was shattered.

"What the hell?" Alliard said, looking around.

"They must've shattered the wards. That mixed with those monsters infecting everything they touch..." I trailed off, shaking my head.

Alliard's demeanor changed as he grew more serious. "We'll move slowly and stick together. Everyone keep their eyes and ears open. The last thing we need is to get ambushed or walk straight into a group of these things because we got careless."

And that's exactly what we did. We took things one step at a time, watching everything around us. We slipped into alleyways when we could since it was safer than staying on the main roads or sidewalks. This allowed me to look at everything and see what damage had been done. For the most part, everything looked normal and untouched. This put me more on edge. They'd been so quick to destroy everything before, so why weren't they doing it now?

"Do any of you know how Drystan escaped?" Alliard asked quietly. "He was handcuffed and surrounded by guards, then had to walk past all of you."

The female guard who argued with me earlier spoke up first, "It all happened so quickly. One second we were watching him being dragged out kicking and screaming and the next second we were being surrounded by those creatures watching him walk out of the front doors."

"We all tried grabbing him, but we were quickly overrun. We had no other choice but to let him go and focus on killing. We hoped another guard would be able to grab him," Someone else added. "Then as we were getting rid of the last of the creatures, Queen Morana walked out of the office. We were all too shocked by what we saw in the office to even think about going after her. We all froze and we shouldn't have. We'll forever be sorry for that."

I shook my head. "At that point, I don't think anyone would have expected you to try to go after her. And honestly, I'm glad you didn't. Who knows how many more lives we would've lost if you had tried arresting or attacking her."

We reached the end of an alleyway forcing us back out onto the sidewalk. Slowly, we rounded a corner only to be met with a small group of creatures sniffing around. As quietly as we could, we unsheathed our weapons and prepared to attack.

"Six by my count," Alliard whispered.

"They're the smaller creatures. They'll be easy to take out," I added.

"Everyone take one. Go for the head," Alliard ordered.

We rushed toward them, attacking in unison. We sliced through their necks, cutting off their heads. Their heads dropped to the ground and rolled. A moment later, their bodies slumped to the ground creating a small pile. We stepped over their bodies and rounded the corner revealing where we'd ended up. Downtown.

I braced myself to see a horrific, bloody scene. Once again, however, everything looked pristine. Well, aside from every plant and bird being dead.

"No guards," Alliard pointed out.

"They have to be in the neighborhoods helping get citizens into the palace," I said. At least, I hoped that's where they were.

"Are Drystan and Morana even still here? Because I feel like we should have seen some sign of them by now," The female guard said.

"They have to still be here," I replied.

"Think Feyre," Alliard said. "Where would they go?"

I shook my head. "I don't know."

"You're the one who pieced all of this together. You know them better than you think you do. You know where they'd go. Just think," he insisted.

I bit the inside of my cheek, running through everything. Luckily, I didn't have to go very far to find my answer.

"The dorioya tree," I blurted.

Alliard's eyes widened with realization. "The dorioya tree."

The guards glanced at one another but didn't ask any questions. Alliard led us into the next alleyway, which would pass by the park where the tree sat. We moved as slowly as we did before. I was now fearful that we'd run into more creatures.

We stopped between two buildings where we could see the tree. There stood Morana and Drystan. They were watching a group of the smaller monsters attack the tree. Two of the larger ones stood on either side of the pair. They looked like

27.

guards.

The glow of the tree was already starting to dim, but there was something different happening too. The once silvery leaves were shifting color becoming more violet.

"Spread out and take out any creatures you come across. Get in position and watch my back," I ordered.

"I'm not letting you walk over there alone," Alliard said.

"And I'm not risking you getting hurt again," I argued.

"Feyre, you cannot go in there without backup."

I couldn't. And it would look suspicious if I walked in there without him hot on my heels since he'd been with me through most of this.

"Alright," I said. "Everyone else, get somewhere you can see us and be ready to jump in when we need you."

We waited until the four guards had disappeared from our sight, then Alliard and I walked out of the alleyway. I exchanged my swords for a set of throwing knives. As we walked, I hurled them at the creatures attacking the dorioya tree. The knives landed in the back of their heads. They fell off the planter, dead. Morana and Drystan whipped around, scouring the area. It only took them a second to spot us walking into the park.

"Well, well, well. What have we here?" Morana said as we approached.

"I expected you to be far away from here by now," Drystan said, sounding amused.

"You think I'm going to let you waltz into my Kingdom with your horrific little army and then just run away?" I asked. "You two really are dumber than you look."

"You should be coming to show us some kindness and gratitude for allowing you to live," Morana said.

Drystan locked eyes with me. "My offer still stands, Feyre.

We can all walk out of here right now."

I formed two new knives and said, "You know, being an only child has made me terrible at sharing. This is your last chance to call this whole thing off and get the hell out of my Kingdom before I'm forced to escalate things."

Morana smirked. "You haven't been formally crowned which leaves Reidell in limbo. Because of that, I, as a Council member and the Queen of Moroluma, will be taking over until that can be done."

That was the last straw for me. They both know exactly what they were doing from the moment they stepped into the palace. I wasn't going to let it go on any longer. I threw both knives at Drystan. One landed in his shoulder and the other was embedded into his chest. I knew it wouldn't be deep enough to pierce his heart, but it certainly gave them a scare. I hoped that would be enough of a signal for the guards to get ready to jump in.

Morana quickly jumped in to help a now panicking Drystan. They started bickering over whether or not they should pull the knives out. I took this time to form my swords and lunge at Morana. I swung one toward her neck while I thrust the other into her stomach. I was able to get her in the stomach, but before I could make contact with her neck, she caught the blade with her hand. I put more pressure on my sword trying to slice through her hand, but my sword wouldn't budge. It was as if I'd hit a brick wall.

"You stupid little bitch!" Morana screeched, shoving my sword away from her. "I tried being nice! I tried letting you live! And now you've wasted both opportunities!"

The shove was so forceful that I almost lost my balance. Alliard was quick to steady me before I got the chance to fall. I prepared myself to strike again but was distracted by my sword that had pierced her. It wasn't coated in red blood. It was thick and black like her creations.

That distraction proved to be detrimental.

Morana snapped her fingers, opening portals on either side of us. Waves of creatures rushed out, both big and small. I saw the guards bolt out of their hiding places, scattering themselves throughout the park. They all looked ready for a fight.

We were quickly swarmed. I wasn't able to see the other guards anymore. I couldn't even see Morana and Drystan. It was just Alliard and I, back to back, attacking everything around us that moved. We were outnumbered, but that wasn't going to deter us.

After a few minutes, we hadn't made a dent in them. For every creature killed, three more took its place.

"We can't stay here!" I shouted. "We need to find the other guards and get out of here!"

"How are we even going to find them in this mess?" Alliard shouted back.

"I don't know!"

I felt myself panicking and I was losing focus. I couldn't let myself do that. I couldn't go down that path. I needed to figure out a way to stay calm and keep my head clear.

As I took a few deep breaths, I heard a gust of wind. I looked over my shoulder and saw Alliard had created a wind tunnel, shoving the creatures out of the way and giving us a path. He grabbed my hand and dragged me behind him. I exchanged my swords for knives once more and started throwing them at every creature in sight. Alliard's wind was strong enough to keep them away, but I didn't want to take any chances.

Still, the creatures were never-ending. Even if we were able to locate the guards, it would be impossible to form a portal in this mess. If we managed to, there was no way we'd get out of here unscathed or without some creatures following us through.

Everything was working against us and my confidence was wavering. I started to think that we wouldn't make it out of this alive.

28.

Bodies were piling up quickly from the ones I was able to kill. Alliard was having no luck finding any signs of the guards. There weren't any flashes of magic. We couldn't hear any of them screaming. There weren't any pieces of their armor or their weapons on the ground. For all we knew, they were already dead and we'd unknowingly stepped over their corpses.

"I know you want to find the other guards, but there's too many of these things for us to keep searching! We're just putting you more at risk!" Alliard shouted over the snarls and growls.

"It's impossible to make a portal here unless we want to let these things into another Kingdom!" I replied.

"I can try to make a bigger clearing! Keep killing and injuring as many as you can and stay close to me!"

I opened my mouth to reply, but something hit me in the back, cutting me off. One of them had managed to get its hand through the wind tunnel. I wasn't injured thanks to my cloak, but it pushed me forward putting me in reach of more creatures. I tried to stop myself only to end up tripping over my own feet, sending me falling to the ground.

"Feyre!"

I hit the ground, barely catching myself with my hands. I braced myself for claws to rip my arms to shreds, but nothing touched me. A moment later, a pair of legs came into my field of view. I looked up and there stood Morana with one of the larger creatures standing behind her. It was blocking the clearing they'd made.

"Are you done being difficult?" Morana asked. She sounded as if she were a mother talking to her child who was throwing a tantrum.

"Not until you're dead," I snapped.

Morana sighed. "This is what I get for trying to be nice."

She motioned a creature forward. It grabbed me by the back of my neck, careful to not touch me with its claws. It lifted me up and walked through the crowd following behind Morana.

"I'd suggest you not struggle. We wouldn't want you getting accidentally hurt or killed," Morana said, sounding bored.

We returned to the base of the dorioya tree. Drystan was there with a sour look on his face. Next to him stood four more creatures, each holding one of the guards. They were still alive and struggling. A creature holding Alliard joined them.

"Now. I was hoping that this would get to be a big reveal for you and the other pathetic Council members, but it seems you've left me no choice but to give you a personal show," Morana said. She looked down at Drystan. "Give me the syringes."

Without any hesitation, Drystan pulled a tin out of his pocket. He popped it open, revealing a handful of syringes filled with a dark, shimmering liquid. Drystan carefully took one out and put it in her hand. She took the safety cap off, exposing the needle. Morana flicked the side to remove any air bubbles and stuck the needle into one of the guard's necks. She pushed the plunger down and I could see the black liquid making its way through his veins.

Morana removed the needle and tossed the syringe aside. Drystan handed her another, and she repeated the process with each guard. Then she reached Alliard. She glanced at me, her eyes swirling with a sick sort of pleasure.

"Leave him alone!" I shouted, now struggling against the creature. "Don't fucking touch him! Leave him alone!"

The creature holding me dug the tips of its claws into the sides of my neck. It was a silent threat that got me to stop moving. Morana pushed the needle into his neck and injected him with the liquid.

One by one, patches of their skin began turning black. They all seized for a moment and their eyes rolled back into their heads. My heart raced as I waited to see what came next.

After what felt like an eternity, they started moving again. Their eyes snapped open in unison and were completely black now. The creatures holding them dropped them and they each landed on their feet with ease. They looked a bit confused but didn't seem panicked or worried at all.

"Wha...what did you do to them?" I asked.

Ignoring me, Morana spoke to Drystan, "They don't look entirely human-like we hoped, but it is the closest we've gotten."

"The real test will be if they stay this way or evolve," Drystan replied.

I started struggling again. The creature did its best to stop me, but I didn't stop this time. It dug its claws deeper into my neck, drawing blood. I encased my hand with aether and dug my own nails into the creature's hand. It was near impossible to get through the skin, but once I did the creature let out a hiss as it loosened its grip. Wiggling a bit more, I was able to get it to let me go. I hid the ground, though it wasn't as gracefully as the guards and Alliard had. I landed in a crouch on my feet but had to firmly plant my fingertips on the ground to steady myself.

"What. The hell. Did. You. Do. To. Them?" I repeated.

"I suppose you could say that we've given them a gift," Morana answered, still not looking at me. "Not a perfect gift, but a gift nonetheless. They'll now be able to wield dark energy as Drystan and I do, as well as the powers they were born with. They'll be more powerful than they've ever been before."

"But…that's…how…" I couldn't form a proper sentence.

That shouldn't be possible. You can't pass powers onto someone. You can't change someone's powers or add to them. Our powers were embedded in our DNA. Nothing could change them or morph them into something new unless it happened naturally.

There were stories throughout our history of people trying to do things like this, but they all ended as complete and utter failures. Each ended in a lot of dead test subjects. The ones doing the experiments either committed suicide or were arrested.

"As soon as we perfect it a bit more, we're going to give everyone in Etrayus this gift," Drystan said. "Our citizens need something better than what these guards received and certainly something better than what those criminals received." He then looked at me. "You could always join us. I mean, imagine what your aether mixed with our dark energy could create. Imagine how much power you could wield."

My eyes ran across all the guards. I silently apologized for what had been done to them and for getting them into this mess. I locked eyes with Alliard. I tried to imagine them as the brown eyes I'd grown to love.

Not looking away from him, I said, "I'd rather die than be one of your puppets."

I had to have imagined it, but I thought I saw Alliard give me a small nod of approval.

"What a shame," Morana sighed. "Don't worry though, we'll try to do something useful with your body."

Without any other words, Morana and Drystan turned and began walking away. Alliard and the other guards followed close behind. I didn't have time to react because the creatures surrounded me again. They didn't waste any time starting their attack and neither did I.

The first group was easy enough for me to take out, but I quickly became overwhelmed. There wasn't anyone here to help or watch my back anymore.

The first hit I got from behind was again blocked by my cloak and this time I was able to keep myself steady. I continued swinging my swords, slicing off heads and injuring them as much as I could. I was moving fast, but not fast enough.

Another set of claws hit me in my side. I was mid-swing and already a bit off-balance, so it sent me to the ground. I didn't hit the ground but instead landed on the dead body of a creature. I tried getting to my feet, but they quickly closed in on me leaving me no room to do so.

I tried to scramble back, but it only moved me closer to the monsters behind me. Then, I felt it. A set of claws dug into my leg. Another sliced open my chest where my cloak had fallen open. Then another went into my upper stomach.

It didn't take long for my body to grow weak and tired.

Darkness began creeping into the edges of my vision. I felt numb now.

The darkness closed in around me. I tried blinking hard, hoping that would get it to retreat. It did nothing. Soon there was no more struggling or moving. There was no more pain. It was over. I had lost.

A flash of white blinded me for a millisecond, then darkness consumed me.

29.

When I came to, I saw my parents. They were far away, but I could still see the sad smiles on their faces. While I wanted to grieve the loss of my own life, I couldn't help but feel overjoyed seeing my parents again. I started running toward them with tears streaming down my face. Just as they were within my reach, I fell.

The next time I awoke, I jolted up. A quick inspection of my surroundings told me I was in a hospital room. Looking down, I saw the bandages on my chest. As I took in a deep breath, I felt the bandages around my torso and there were more wrapped around my legs and thighs. There was an IV in my hand and all I could hear was the irritating beeping of the heart rate monitor.

As I started searching for the 'call nurse' button, Merindah walked into the room with a cup in her hand. When she saw me up and alert, her eyes widened and she dropped the cup on the ground rushing over to me. She gently pulled me into a hug. Tears were already falling from her eyes.

"Thank god, thank god, thank god," She whispered. Before I could react, she pulled away and ran back over to the door. She peaked her head out and shouted, "Get Queen Amara and Queen Csilla in here now!" Then she returned to my side, settling into a chair that was next to the bed.

The scene gave me flashbacks to when Alliard and I were attacked. My chest grew tight and I had to quickly blink the tears away. A moment later, Amara and Csilla stepped into the room. Both became visibly relieved when they saw me.

"Eos and Demir are busy building up the wards in Dradour, but I'm sure as soon as they're free they'll be here for a visit," Amara said.

"What's going on? How long have I been out?" I asked.

"Feyre, don't you think you should try to rest a bit more before jumping into business?" Merindah asked.

"No," I said firmly. "I need to know now. Please."

Csilla and Amara exchanged a quick glance, silently communicating. I'm sure they too agreed with Merindah.

"I need to hear this now before I fall into whatever mental breakdown I'm sure I'm going to have when my brain has time to process everything. So, please. I need to know."

Letting out a small sigh, Csilla began talking, "Reidell and Artheas have both fallen. Felluna's wards stayed strong and the dark energy hasn't been able to make it up to Dradour yet. We're putting up wards there as a precaution because we cannot risk losing another Kingdom. We have also evacuated all cities and towns."

"As for you," Amara said. "You've only been out for a few days. The doctors and Elders weren't sure you'd recover at all because your injuries were so bad, but they refused to give up."

"How did I get here, though?" I asked.

"When reinforcements arrived, they began searching for you. They didn't run into any of those monsters so they were able to reach the park quickly. They thinned out the hoard that was there and were able to find you. Eos let out a burst of aether, it blinded and stunned the creatures long enough for them to get you out of there," Csilla answered.

The flash of light. It must've been the aether.

"What of the citizens?"

Amara's demeanor changed as she looked away from me. "Only about half of Reidell and Artheas' citizens are accounted for and none from Moroluma. Morana and Drystan have blocked all portals in and out of the Kingdoms so we can't get in there to rescue the remainder of them."

"That means my parents…" I couldn't finish that sentence. Not out loud. If I said it out loud, it made this real. That realization alone would break me.

"I'm sorry Feyre," Amara whispered. "We've tried everything we could to get in there and we've failed every time."

There was a moment of silence between us. That's when I realized they didn't know what happened after Eos left. They didn't know about Alliard and the guards. They had no idea about what Morana and Drystan had done.

I jumped into telling them everything that happened at the park. Each piece of the story shocked them more than the last. When I finished, they looked confused and defeated.

"None of that should be possible," Amara said, shaking her head. "We know based on things that have happened in the past that there's no way to mix, combine, or change someone's powers unless your body does it naturally."

"Well, they've found a way to do it," I replied.

"Even if it were possible, it would take a lot of time and tests to figure it out. How could they get away with any of that with no one knowing?"

"Clearly they've been able to get away with a lot without anyone's knowledge," Merindah stated.

"I'll bring it up to The Elders. They were alive when that man Delroy created Moroluma and was doing all those inhumane tests. If anyone's going to know anything, it's them," Csilla said.

"What are we supposed to do now? How are we supposed to stop them when they have three of our five Kingdoms and who knows how many test subjects at their disposal?" Merindah asked.

"They haven't perfected their 'gift' yet. We have time to figure this out," I said.

While I sounded confident, I didn't feel it. The odds were stacked against us and we were backed into a corner. But I wasn't giving up until Etrayus was ours again.

Acknowledgments

I don't even know where to start with this. I never in a million years thought I'd be writing my own acknowledgments page. But here we are.

I'll start with my family. They've been supporting this dream of mine for almost 10 years. I would never have been able to gain the confidence and determination to follow through with this if it wasn't for them.

Next has to be my amazing boyfriend. Not only has he supported this crazy dream of mine since we met, but he's also been a giant help. He did my cover, he's talked me out of wanting to quit more times than I can count, and he believed in me even when I didn't believe in myself. I truly don't deserve him.

Of course I can't forget my best friend. Without him I wouldn't even have a title for this creation. At least, I wouldn't have one this cool. He's been a massive support since we met and I wouldn't have made it this far without him.

This book also wouldn't have been possible without all the amazing people I've met in the writing community. Without them answering every question I had or offering all of their help and support I would have been more lost than I already was. This book would probably be a giant, jumbled mess without them. They've become amazing friends and I cannot thank them enough for all that they've done for me.

And finally, thank you my dear reader. Thank you for giving my little book a chance. You're helping make my dreams a reality which means more to me than you'll ever know.